Vegas Baby and the Great Red Spot

Vegas Baby and the Great Red Spot

C.R. Ward

"Perspective is everything."
C.R. Ward

"Turn your interest into a passion,
turn your passion into a profit."

C.R. Ward

Chapter 1

The hardest part is always getting started. Vegas Baby had spent weeks tracking a serial killer who had committed at least ten murders in Nevada. It took one week to get a decent lead, another week to connect that lead to a face, and two more weeks to get this close to the murdering bastard. Vegas ran through the streets of Las Vegas chasing the killer who called himself "Killsong." Killsong apparently had the ability to drain a person of all hopes and desires. He could suck away every positive aspect of a person's life until they wanted—until they needed to be put out of their misery. That was one of the reasons it was so hard to track the killer down. He was good—but Vegas Baby was better.

The chase had lasted for almost two miles. It didn't take long for him to realize that this trek was nothing more than an elaborate death trap. Every few steps, another explosion powerful enough to break Vegas' bones and rattle his teeth would go off. Not to mention the snipers Killsong had stationed in different parts of the city waiting to take his head off as soon as they had a clear shot. It was obvious that Killsong had planned this. He had to have known that Vegas was hunting him, so he set a trap turning the hunter into the prey. Vegas hated being the prey!

Vegas felt like his muscles were running off battery acid and his heart was pumping syrup. If it wasn't for the nannites coursing through his veins powered by his own lactic acids, he would have been left bloodied and broken on the back streets with the filth and prostitutes. Even though he wouldn't get tired, Vegas was starting to worry. Killsong had shown off the ability to do all sorts of parkour moves across the city, but he showed no sign of tiring, plus the maze of explosions was getting more and more elaborate. He was able to stay step in step with Killsong but Vegas wondered if he was hot on the tail of a super power villain or if the bastard was just too crazy to know that he should be fucking tired!

Vegas had run across busy city streets, jumped from rooftop to rooftop, and in and out of buildings, was nearly blown up ten times, and killed five snipers before he started to lose his patience. It would have been a big bonus if he could bring this bastard in unharmed, but screw it! While running, Vegas finally reached in his pocket and slid his pink glove over his left hand. Up until now, he had only used the glove to rid himself of the snipers Killsong had targeting him, but things were getting out of hand. He counted at least twelve civilian casualties thanks to Killsong's bombs and the property damage was closing in on the millions!

As soon as the glove was on, Vegas felt it pulsate and crackle with energy as it turned red. He brushed his hands together, linking the power of the glove with his mind and visualized what he wanted. Almost instantly, Vegas felt the weight of a Beretta form in his gloved hand. The glove was Vegas' own creation powered by the same nannites that ran through his blood. However, the nannites in the glove served a much different purpose; they could create almost any weapon Vegas could imagine. The power glove being pink was a little superfluous but it created an edge that he often exploited.

Vegas vaulted though more explosions smelling the C4 and his own burning flesh. He felt the nannites rebuilding his muscles; his fatigue fed the tiny machines, hastening them to keep Vegas on his feet. His anger fueled his drive, refusing to let him quit. Vegas hated being blown up and he hated chasing people, but most of all he hated to lose!

Killsong looked back at Vegas barreling down on him. He had to see Vegas' body charred and bloodied, his clothes tattered and torn almost beyond recognition. Most of all he had to see Vegas' resolve. There was nothing Killsong could do, no level of preparation he could have done to make Vegas give up. Killsong looked back and Vegas locked eyes with him. At that moment Vegas finally saw a crack in Killsong's bravado. Vegas pushed himself harder letting the nannites do their work and pushed away the pain. He waited until Killsong gave him a clear angle. Vegas focused his eyes, linked up with the power in the glove and the gun it created until it was an extension of his own hand and the target was the size of a mountain in his mind's eye. Quickly, confidently, Vegas squeezed the trigger. Killsong screamed in pain and barreled into some trash at the end on the alleyway.

When Vegas caught up to Killsong, he was screaming, scratching, and clawing like a caged animal. The alley was sparsely lit and Vegas struggled to make out the details of Killsong's face through the warped, desolate shadows of the Sin City back alley. Killsong was foaming at the mouth through yellowed, jacked-up teeth and his shoulder length blonde, matted, sweaty hair hung over his eyes. His eyes were pale blue and full of nothing but hate, blood lust and utter contempt for human life.

"You fuck! You really think you're better than me? I know who you are! I know what you've done!" Killsong growled. "Vegas Baby, the savior of Las Vegas, my ass! I know about you. I know what you do. I know about the women you've fucked, the people you killed for money, the drug deals you run! Do you really think you're better than me, you mother fucker?"

Vegas casually looked down on Killsong from the shadows. Vegas could only assume that if he had feelings he would have some sense of pity. Instead Vegas clapped his hands together again and felt the familiar crackle of energy as the Berretta in his hand disappeared. Now that the gun was gone the glove itself was glowing and shooting sparks of ruby energy as Vegas tightened his hand into a fist.

He grabbed Killsong by the throat with his right hand, and then used the gloved hand to illuminate the twisted features of the murderer's countenance. Vegas used his strength to force air out of the killer's lungs with a simple clutching of his hand.

"Of course I'm better than you, idiot," Vegas said forcing Killsong's eyes to his. "Nobody can prove anything that I've done."

He smiled then, with one punch knocking Killsong unconscious, but he immediately regretted it. Now he was going to have to carry this bastard all the way back to the car.

Damnit, Vegas thought, *anger management classes just aren't working.*

* * * *

One more thing done on a never-ending list of things to do, Vegas thought while sitting in his office in North Las Vegas. The office that Vegas ran his entire operation from was more like home than a place of business. Vegas' whole life was in these walls. He sat at his desk and looked over the different jobs he could choose. He had to admit he was pleased that his options were finally starting to grow along with his reputation. There were offers of assassination attempts, finding missing people, drug deals, women offering their bodies to him, people who lost something and needed a get-backer, the job offers went on and on. Vegas even had high profile government contracts on the table.

It had taken years for Vegas to reach the level of notoriety he now enjoyed. To the majority of Las Vegas, he was a hero. But the underbelly of the city knew him for what he sometimes chose to be. Nothing was beneath Vegas as long as the money was right. He was just about to choose another project to stave off the ever-present sense of boredom when a bright crimson light started to emanate from the center of his office. Something began to push out from the light, transparent like wind, but more solid than steel—a force was pushing outward from the light to create room for its presence.

Papers were pushed off Vegas' desk. Furniture was pushed out of place as the atmosphere in the room became thick, making it hard to breath. The light was as blinding as the sun and briefly gave off a heat almost as intense. Suddenly, the presence became more and more familiar until Vegas knew who was paying him a visit. The light disseminated and Vegas was standing face to face with The Chosen One of Legend.

"Hello Vegas," Chosen One said without moving his lips. Vegas looked at him annoyed—almost beyond restraint. Vegas would have lashed out but he quickly remembered how futile it would've been. The Chosen One had shown up in Vegas' home unannounced and didn't even have the courtesy to show up in person. Vegas was staring at an astral projection, a mental image generated by the Chosen One. Vegas could see the Chosen One's caramel colored skin glow in contrast to his ruby eyes. His smooth chiseled features were set in a smugly perfect smile while his flawlessly braided hair hung down to his shoulders. The astral projection was clad in the Chosen One's red and white uniform, his red cape with its white trim hanging down to his calves. One glance and Vegas took in all these details and remembered why he hated this smarmy bitch so much.

"What the fuck are you doing here?" Vegas said not trying to hide his irritation.

"I know you're not my biggest fan Vegas, but I need your help to save the universe," Chosen One again said without moving his lips which only confirmed to Vegas that his mind was being invaded as well as his office.

"Wow, really? Not the city or the planet, but you need me to save the whole damn universe, huh?"

"As a matter of fact, yes I do."

"Well, fuck off and find someone else."

"There is no one else—believe me. If there were, I wouldn't be wasting the last bit of power I have to talk to you."

Vegas chuckled. "Oh, so the Chosen One of Legend does have a limit to his great and magnificent power. I'm shocked!"

"We don't have time for your sarcasm. True, I am the most powerful being you have yet to see in your life. However, even I have my limits. Even now I am engaged in a fight for my life that I might not win, which is forcing me to ask for your help."

Vegas had long since taken precautions against telepaths. Even a telepath as powerful as Chosen One couldn't make Vegas do or say anything he didn't want to, but Vegas couldn't lock them out completely. Telepaths that were powerful enough could still talk in Vegas' head and read some of his thoughts. The worst part is that they could still share their emotions with Vegas. Because of this, Vegas could feel the desperation and fear in the Chosen One's essence. Vegas could feel the panic and the break in the armor of absolute confidence that normally pulsed from the Chosen One. The cocky bastard had been knocked down a peg or two—he really needed Vegas' help. Vegas didn't know if he should celebrate the Chosen One's apparent humiliation or hide under a rock in fear of whatever impending doom had him so shaken.

"Fine!" Vegas barked, caught in between emotions, "What is it you need? And this better be as big as you say. I could be out getting some pussy right now."

"You and me both," Chosen One chuckled, "but believe me, this is utterly important for your universe to survive."

Vegas held down the twinge of provocation he felt. This bastard couldn't help but separate himself from everyone else. He had to throw in the fact that he's from some strange other universe that makes him different—better—and far more powerful than normal people. Like he was a man doing his dogs a favor! Vegas knew that the Chosen One was in his head and knew how he felt, but he didn't care. Instead, he forced his feelings aside and listened to what the Chosen One had to say.

"I don't have all night so start talking."

"I'm afraid it isn't that simple," Chosen One said meekly. "I'm afraid I will have to show you what I'm talking about for you to truly grasp the danger."

"Try me."

"It would be useless, I must summon your own astral projection in order for you to see what I have to show you."

"Bullshit! You just want to get in my head. No! Not happening!"

Chosen One's astral projections glowed bright red with power as he glided toward Vegas, "I wasn't asking your permission, Vegas. You're going to see what I have to show you regardless of what you want."

Before Vegas could respond, the Chosen One reached out with blinding speed as his hand made contact with Vegas' head. Vegas felt his essence, his soul, everything that made Vegas who he was, being ripped from his body. The sensation was like a million needles pricking his skin one after another from head to toe. He tried to fight back, but he was helpless as Chosen One did what should've been impossible. Vegas felt himself become weightless; he felt his consciousness being lifted until—he was looking down at his office, then down on his building, then Nevada, and then down at the country, followed by the whole planet Earth.

Vegas was furious! He hated not being in control. He couldn't stand having his free will stripped away like this. Vegas tried to speak but couldn't.

"I'm sorry, Vegas, but you are here to observe and listen. I don't have time to be gentle with your ego. This isn't how I would have chosen to go about this, but I could feel you weren't going to give me many options and given the time I have, this approach is necessary."

Vegas couldn't speak or even form a conscious thought, but he knew his emotions were still on display for the Chosen One. Vegas made sure his displeasure was known, he let his anger at the Chosen One's audacity fill him, then push outward until he was sure his feelings were shared.

Chosen One bellowed with laughter. "I may be kind, Vegas, but just as my power may have its limits, so does my patience. While I do not wish to offend, do not confuse that with actually caring about your feelings."

Vegas felt Chosen One impose his will over him, and a silent understanding passed between the two. If Vegas kept pushing, Chosen One would just as soon see his mind turned to mush as ask for Vegas' help.

"Now come, Vegas Baby. I'm not sure you can handle everything I'm about to show you, but you are about to have much to do with little time to prepare."

Chapter 2

Vegas Baby felt himself being spirited away against his will behind The Chosen One of Legend. He still couldn't form a conscious thought, but his anger was still on display. Every form of communication had been stripped from Vegas, but he still had the ability to process information. He tried to ignore Chosen One. Vegas didn't want to hear a word he had to say, but he was helpless. He had no choice but to float aimlessly and absorb all the information Chosen One presented.

"There is a lot you need to see in order to fully grasp what is happening, but I don't have enough power or time to show you everything. So you will have to fill in the blanks on your own. The first thing you need to know is some fundamental facts about your universe.

"What you first need to see may be the most difficult for you to believe, but I am forced to start there due to my time constraints."

Vegas' spirit trailed Chosen One as he talked without looking back. As he finished speaking, light from the stars seemed to warp and twist into strange shapes and colors until the light formed a spiraling tunnel. The sensation was something Vegas had never felt before. It was as though he was his own center of gravity and stood still while the horizon rushed to meet him. The sensation just wasn't natural; Vegas felt as though his soul was being wrenched and distorted. His mind felt as though it was teetering on the edge of sanity, he wanted to scream, he wanted to escape, but then when he felt himself pushed to the limit—the experience ended as suddenly as it began.

Vegas struggled to get his bearings when he saw the Earth scuttling towards him. Vegas saw the continent of Africa, and then the northern end of the continent was pushed into view, followed by Egypt. However, the Egypt Vegas now saw wasn't the one he knew, rather a version of the country as it would have been thousands of years ago. Vegas saw the Nile River, the Sphinx, and the Great Pyramids of Giza all appearing with more pristine glory than Vegas could have even imagined. There were colors and designs Egyptologists hadn't even considered. There were hieroglyphs telling stories long erased from history.

For a brief moment, Vegas almost felt excited about his abduction. Being able to view ancient Egypt like this was practically worth it!

"I apologize, Vegas, but this isn't what I had to show you. I brought you here so that you could be better prepared for what comes next. I know you have a reverence for things of Egyptian descent—come. There is still much you need to see and accept as reality," Chosen said grimly.

Suddenly Vegas was ripped away from the hieroglyphs he was deciphering and forced into the most magnificent Egyptian temple he had ever seen. Vegas wasn't familiar with the temple, so he knew it had to be either undiscovered or it had been destroyed before his time. Vegas wanted to see the outside of the temple to get some sense of its location, but knew he wouldn't get the chance.

Before Vegas could become angry all over again, he noticed the people—or rather the beings—in the temple. Vegas saw a young, strong, regal looking man standing before a throne addressing servants. Despite all the wonders of the hieroglyphs, jewelry, decorations, and all of the lost history to view, Vegas' eyes were transfixed on the king. For some reason, he looked more than human. Vegas tried but couldn't form the thoughts needed to figure out which Pharaoh he was gazing upon. Vegas focused his eyes more and seemed to see both the Pharaoh and another entity superimposed on him, one with bronzed glowing skin with the head of a falcon. Then Vegas noticed the unmistakable symbol behind the god-king. It was the eye of Horus—Vegas was looking at the Egyptian god Horus!

As Vegas scanned the room, he discerned more and more symbols and more gods in the temple. It was only now that Vegas noticed that standing beside Horus was the most beautifully majestic woman he had ever seen in his life. From her clothes, jewelry, and brilliant wings under her human arms, it was easy for Vegas to identify her as Isis the Egyptian god of magic!

"That's right Vegas. I wanted you to see this and believe. The Egyptian gods are real. They still exist in your time, all be it in a state of eternal sleep. There are many secrets about your universe that humans are not close to grasping. If you succeed in the mission I am about to place before you and save your universe, I will reveal some of these secrets to you fully.

"This is the first step in your understanding. There is still more you must see and believe—come."

* * * *

Once more Vegas felt himself being yanked away. He felt his sanity being stretched to its limits as light twisted and warped around him again. Once the psychic maelstrom subsided, Vegas could tell he was floating above another ancient city but wasn't sure which one. Vegas hadn't studied all ancient cultures as carefully as the Egyptians. Seconds passed before Vegas spotted an enormous wall around the city and an incredible battle waging within the walls. Vegas' eye was drawn towards a giant wooden horse and suddenly he knew where he was. He was observing the battle of Troy! It wasn't long before Vegas saw a warrior that stood out among the other soldiers. He was clad in brazen armor covered in dirt and blood from his enemies. Everyone in the warrior's path was cut down just as quickly as they rose to challenge him. The warrior's technique was flawless, no movement was wasted, every swing of his shield blocked an incoming attack, and every slash of his sword eviscerated his adversary. Vegas could feel the warrior's bloodlust—his quest for eternal glory. The warrior could be no other than Achilles.

"Very good, Vegas. It pleases me that you are able to piece these scenes together without me having to explain them to you. This is the storied battle of Troy, and that is Achilles in all of his grandeur. We must move—our time is growing short. I can not stay in the time stream much longer and you have two more things to see."

Again, Vegas was made to follow as Chosen One ascended into the heavens. Vegas expected the twisting of light and the tug on his sanity again but instead was met with a large mountain that seemed to be floating in the sky. Vegas felt Chosen One speed up as the enormous mound of earth and rock zoomed by until they sommitted the mountain.

Atop the mountain, Vegas saw a giant towering over the edge, standing proud and strong as he surveyed all that was below him. The giant had silver hair that hung below his massive shoulders and a beard of matching silver down to his chest. He was dressed in a long cloth that flowed down his ankles and across his chest exposing muscles that looked carved of some glossy tanned colored rock. The giant's eyes pulsed with the power and fury of a thousand thunderstorms. Vegas instantly was struck with astonishment from looking at Zeus—the Greek god of thunder.

"Again you impress me, Vegas. You are accepting the images of the past much quicker than I would have expected. Now let us take our leave before we are noticed."

Vegas experienced a different sensation as Chosen One zipped them back to the present. Instead of a pull and twist, it was more like a shift in their position. Yet, as they were leaving, Vegas noticed Zeus's eyes faintly look in his direction. The power Vegas saw in the thunder god's eyes was enough to strike him with a fear that he had never known. It wasn't like Zeus was looking at Vegas, but rather looking through him until he held no secrets. Vegas was filled with a brief but intense terror at the thunder god noticing his presence. The exchange only lasted an instant, but it would stay with Vegas for the rest of his life. Suddenly, Vegas' mind's eye blinked and he was looking at the fifth planet in the solar system, the Jovian giant—Jupiter.

Vegas had studied the planets and he had an extensive knowledge of Jupiter, but nothing could prepare him for seeing the gas giant up close. Vegas calculated that in their current position, they were floating as far from Jupiter as the moon was from Earth. At that distance Earth would look like it could fit in the palm of your hand; however, Jupiter still dwarfed Vegas' field of vision. Vegas could see most of Jupiter's sixty seven moons, the beautiful auras created by the planet's massive magnetosphere, and the most interesting feature sat directly in front of Vegas—the great red spot—and anti cyclonic hurricane over three times larger than the planet Earth.

As Vegas took in his surroundings, Chosen One spoke. Vegas wanted to block him out and try to process everything he was seeing, but the Chosen One's voice was predominant in his mind.

"I apologize again. It is much easier to exit the time stream than to enter and travel through it. You are now looking at the planet Jupiter as it exists in the present. The next thing I have to show you is the reason I have abducted you, and however unbelievable, I assure you it is one hundred percent real."

The next thing Vegas knew, he was zooming towards the great red spot, diving deeper and deeper into the center of the largest storm in the solar system. Even descending at such high speeds into the center of the storm, it was still a mass of chaos and violence. Swirling colors of oranges, reds, pinks, browns and whites were pushed in every direction, and lightning bigger than some states in North America flashed. As they slowed, Vegas struggled to make out a massive structure that seemed to not only be the center of the storm but its source of power. Vehemence and energy seemed to pump in and out of the structure like blood to a heart. Vegas couldn't think of the word to describe the structure. It wasn't exactly a stadium, or coliseum; the sheer scale of it seemed to defy laws of physics. He couldn't see it clearly from the distance where Chosen One had decided to stop, but it gave off a dark scarlet glow. The only thing Vegas was sure of was that it couldn't have been formed naturally. No structure should be able to stand under the enormous pressure of Jupiter's surface. Vegas still had trouble forming a decent thought, but he did wonder why Chosen One had stopped so far from whatever it was he was now looking at. If this is what Vegas was suppose to see, why was he not allowed to see it in detail?

"There are powers at work here beyond my ability to defeat in my current state. Any closer and our presence would be detected," Chosen One said responding to Vegas' silent concerns. "Everything I have shown you was to help you to understand that this place does exist. You are the only human to ever see the temple of the Titans. I don't have time to explain, but the gods are still alive—their influence over humans weakened but still alive.

"Inside this crimson temple is a power unequal to anything else in your galaxy— perhaps the entire universe. A power even the gods and Titans fear. What you must do Vegas: Find a way to reach this structure on Jupiter's surface, defeat any obstacles in your path, and steal this power from the Titans that you will need to save the universe."

Vegas listened to the Chosen One of Legend and felt the anxiety and truth in his voice. Vegas could also feel the Chosen One's power fading because he was able to form cohesive thoughts again. Vegas instantly began running calculations and scenarios. He wasn't sure if Chosen One was manipulating him or not, but he was intrigued by the challenge more than anything now. The prospect of pulling off something of this magnitude, to stare at the face of the impossible and succeed, to accomplish a task no other person could even comprehend, was the type of thing Vegas dreamed of. But why-- why was Vegas acquiring this power so important? For it to matter, in order to obtain absolute glory for his deed the ends had to justify the means. A mission like this is worthless without the proper reason to accomplish it.

"You must forgive me," Chosen One said pulling Vegas from his thoughts, "but our time is up. I do not have the power to continue this if I am to get you back to your body."

Vegas looked at Chosen One and saw him look much different than he did when he first appeared. His uniform of red and white was torn and shredded and caked in blood in places. Chosen One had lacerations all over his body; his perfectly braided hair was in shambles, even torn out in clumps in places. The most disturbing thing Vegas noticed was Chosen One's eyes. They were bursting with an energy that Vegas thought may have surpassed what he had seen in Zeus just moments before.

Chosen One looked directly at Vegas and spoke his final words: "Because of your petulance, I left you a surprise back at your body. But the crux of the matter is that Gor is being resurrected, Vegas! Look at the center of your galaxy to find the reason for your quest. Good luck, Vegas Baby, you have exactly six months to acquire the power—if you fail, it will be the end of everything."

Suddenly, Vegas sprung awake gasping for air. His eyes were full of tears, his muscles were stinging as if spikes were stabbing him, making the slightest move painful. Vegas waited until he was able to catch his breath and composure. He was able to recount everything that had happened. He remembered every detail of every image. Vegas knew what he had to do—as soon as he was able to stand.

Once Vegas was strong enough, he stood and did a body check to make sure he was okay. Then he smelled something terrible and felt something wet.

After examining himself, Vegas was filled with anger as he discovered the Chosen One's 'surprise'. He had set Vegas up; he had done it on purpose with his telekinesis! While he was away from his body, Vegas had shit himself.

"Son of a bitch!"

Chapter 3

Vegas sighed deeply and looked around his office where he had assembled his friends. Each of them were very different from one other and had special abilities just as unique. There was Joe Warfield, Jen, Panda Jack, Topaz, Zo, Blu Mbagwu, Robert Holley, and Deep Willis.

"You really expect us ta buy that load of horse shit you sell'n," Rob said after taking another gulp of his beer. Rob stood 6'6" wearing his favorite blue jeans and white wife beater which showcased his muscular frame forged from years of mining.

"Why would I lie about something this big?" Vegas replied.

"The same reason you lie about everything else; you're a fucking liar!" Topaz barked from where she stood in the corner of the office. Her arms folded and legs crossed, she was one of the most beautiful women Vegas had ever been around. She wore a dark gray hooded sweatshirt that was cut just below her perfect breast and a pair of matching baggy sweat pants that hid her shape. Vegas didn't mind; he had every inch of Topaz committed to memory. Topaz had a body to die for: thick brown wavy hair, creamy caramel skin with blue eyes that were a gaudy side affect of her abilities. Despite her looks, Vegas wondered if inviting her was a good idea given their recent history.

"Is it really too much to ask that you be mature enough to put our past behind us long enough to save the universe?" Vegas snapped back, "Your powers would be extremely helpful."

"Well, I, for one, definitely didn't come here ta hear ya two argue." Zo cut in with his thick Jamaican accent, stretching his muscles as his Rastafarian clothes hung loose over his golden brown body. Zo ran a hand through his shoulder length dreads looking extremely disinterested in the conversation.

"I agree with Zolomon," Panda Jack growled from the corner where he was encased in shadow. "I suggest we all stay on topic. The sooner Vegas finishes saying his piece, the sooner we can all leave." Panda Jack glared at Vegas with the dark circles under his eyes that inspired his surname. Panda adjusted his long dusty brown trench coat retreating deeper into the shadows.

"Amen," Blu chimed in with her sensual African accent from where she sat on Vegas' desk. Vegas had always admired Blu's style. She had smooth ebony skin, petite breasts, thick thighs and ass from her time as an Olympic track star, and full seductive lips she often augmented with lipstick and smoky eye shadow. Vegas wanted to know her on a more intimate level but had never had to opportunity to try. It wasn't surprising he wasn't able to get Blu to stay still long enough to make a move considering she could almost run at the speed of light. People who see her in her uniform know her best as Bluestreak.

Jen stood from his seat pulling himself to his full height of 5'6" and addressed the group. His voice carried wisdom beyond his twenty-three years: "You pulled in favors to get us all here, Vegas. I really hope you have some proof because your story seems pretty unbelievable."

"Are you guys serious? I told you what happened. The Chosen One of Legend showed up and did some cosmic-voodoo-time shit. All of you are just going to have to believe me."

Deep was next to speak as he adjusted his glasses and massaged his neatly trimmed beard, "I want to believe you, Vegas, but your track record with these matters is somewhat—dubious. Plus, your story raises a lot of questions. You and The Chosen One have never really had a great relationship. Why would he appear to you instead of one of us?"

Of all the people in the room, Vegas respected Professor Deep Willis the most. Deep had dark brown skin, stood 6'0" and was built like a tank—nonetheless he was one of the leading professors at UNLV.

"He said he didn't have a lot of energy—for whatever reason I'm not really sure. If he survives whatever he's going through, then you can ask him yourself. I just know what I'm telling you is true," Vegas remarked.

Rob had finished the last of his beer and was getting another out of Vegas' mini fridge. "The proof is always in the pudd'n—so where's the pudd'n?"

"Vegas, you're going to have to show them. This pack of ingrates ain't gonna believe shit if you don't." Joe said with irritation in his voice.

"There isn't much to show," Vegas said. "I really need you guys to understand that I need your help."

"In other words you don't have any proof," Topaz shot.

"I didn't say that, just that it isn't much."

"I'm sorry, Vegas, but you're going to have to give us something. If the Chosen One was here to back you up, it would be a different story because your word doesn't carry a lot of weight," Deep said regrettably.

"Wow really? Is that how it is? After everything I've individually done for all of you, and you still need proof when I come to you with something this big?"

There was a brief pause as everyone in the room examined each other.

"Yeah," everyone ultimately said in unison. Vegas paused looking shocked. He couldn't believe they had such little trust in him. Vegas looked as if he had been betrayed—cut deeper than any blade could go.

"Fine! If that's what it takes to get any of you to help save the damn universe, then I'll show you what I have. But remember just because it isn't much, doesn't mean it isn't real!" Vegas snapped.

Vegas kept a look of betrayal and anger as he reached into his pocket and pulled out a small handheld device. Vegas was sure he looked upset to everyone in the room although in reality, Vegas was using all his strength not to smile. He expected everyone to not trust him. After all, he was an asshole most of the time. This was all part of the grand scheme of things in Vegas' plans for his "friends." They didn't need to trust, or even like him—yet. The main thing at this stage was that they all respected him and that respect is what got them to come when called.

The device Vegas pulled out of his pocket was round, about the size of a golf ball on top, and shaped like a tripod on the bottom. Vegas walked to the center of the room and placed the device on the carpet. Then he walked to a nearby cabinet where he pulled out several pairs of thick gray goggles. The goggles were bulky and made to encircle a person's entire field of vision when pulled over the eyes.

"Everyone put one of these on," Vegas said without looking at anyone still sounding upset. Vegas took one for himself and then passed the others around the room.

Rob took the gray goggles, another swig of his beer, then began, "Aw, come on Vegas, you know we don't mean any—"

"It's fine Rob." Vegas cut him off.

There was a silence in the room that resonated louder than any scream could. Deep got his goggles and then tried to cut through the tension. "Vegas you have to understand that—"

"I said it was fine!" Vegas spat. "Just put on the damn goggles."

There was another awkward silence as everyone hesitated to put on their goggles.

"I'm sorry, but I can't do this," Blu said looking distastefully at the goggles in her hand.

Vegas sighed annoyed. "You can't do what, Blu? What the fuck can't you do?"

"I can't wear this thing! It's ugly!" Blu was serious, but she was also able to say it in a way that made everyone chuckle. Just a couple of words and a smirk on her luscious red lips was all Blu needed to pull one and all from the edge and elevate tension in a room. "I mean do you see how cute I look right now, Vegas? You see this outfit."

Blu was decked in red skinny jeans with a form fitting black shirt showing every curve of her Olympic-built torso. Her hair was in a multitude of two-inch twists, the first stage of dreadlocks she always wanted to grow but couldn't due to her track career. Blu looked classy, approachable, sexy, and flirty all at once. With one glance Vegas could have painted a picture of her with ostentatious detail.

Vegas grunted sarcastically, "I was busy trying to convince everybody that the universe was in danger, so no Blu, I haven't noticed your outfit."

Blu slowly took off her scarlet patent leather platform pumps. "Your loss. If all of you will excuse me for just two seconds."

With a flash of blue lighting, Blu disappeared. Everyone barely had a chance to blink before she reappeared almost as though she hadn't left. She even had her red pumps back on. In her hands were the goggles, but they were now painted a reddish-pink hue and had black trim that matched her outfit flawlessly.

"All right. Sorry it took so long, but it's hard to run in these pants. Now I'm ready," Blu announced crossing her arms and showing her pearly whites.

The group paused, trying to process what Blu had done until Rob broke the stillness. "How'd ya get da paint to dry that fast?"

Everyone laughed. Vegas noticed with the burden of talking about the destruction of the universe brought, the assemblage of heroes was happy to seize the light-hearted moment. Everyone but Panda Jack, that is.

Vegas didn't see any hint of a grin on Panda's face. Instead, he looked as though he were grinding his teeth. Vegas remembered that while he had everyone else pretty much pegged with at least some idea, if not total knowledge, of how their powers worked, Christopher "Panda Jack" Nelson was still a huge question mark. Panda stayed in the shadows sequestered from the group. With deep age lines etched in his face, silver hair pulled into tight ponytail with his brown duster trench coat and clothes straight out of an old cowboy western, Panda looked like a man from another time. He always seemed out of touch with his surroundings and either uninterested or irritated by people around him.

"Okay, Vegas. Whatever you have to show us, let's do it already. I got a new girl running the register at my record store and I need to get back before something happens," Jen said pulling Vegas from his thoughts.

"Suits me. Everyone put on your goggles—please."

One by one the group did as they were asked.

"Topaz, could you cut off the lights for me?"

"Why do you need me to do it?"

"Because—you're—closest."

Topaz mumbled to herself and glared at Vegas. Then she pointed at the light switch as the blue earrings she wore began to glow faintly. Vegas watched as Topaz focused the power she pulled from the regular jewelry she wore. After a brief second, the power of telekinesis flowed from the jewelry, through her body, finally flicking the light switch.

Vegas glanced in Jen's direction and noticed a glimpse of pride on his face. Jen had spent a lot of time and effort teaching Topaz to control her powers with that amount of finesse. Jen was also known as the Human Weapon, thanks to his mastery of his chi, the flow of energy in the body. That ability, coupled with the ability to tap into the energy of every living thing around him made Jen one of the most powerful beings on the planet and the perfect person to help Topaz control her unique powers. Vegas tried to test Topaz once to understand how she was able to draw power from jewelry and why different stones gave her different abilities. Diamonds would give her one power, opals would give her another, and rubies would let her do something completely different and so on.

Vegas pushed that puzzle of ambiguity from his mind and reached into his pocket pulling out his power glove and placed it on his left hand. Then he clapped his hands together, felt the familiar crackle of energy and linked the glove with his mind forcing it to form what he imagined. In an instant, Vegas was wearing two thick gray electronic gloves with glowing red sensors on each fingertip.

"Yo, mon, does mine be broken? Cause I'm not see'n a ting," Zo said.

"Yeah, what gives? I'm afraid of the dark," Rob joked.

"Vegas, if this is one of your bullshit pranks, I swear to God."

"Topaz baby, chill. I just need a second to fire this thing up. I made it myself you know."

"Nothing you make is impressive to me anymore, and don't call me baby."

"Damn," Joe cut in, "girl you need to get laid!"

That got a giggle out of a few people including Vegas. Before Topaz could deliver her colorful responses, Vegas clapped his hands together again, the device on the floor clicked on and the room exploded in swirling lights and shapes.

"Everybody step back," Vegas, broadcasted. "I don't want anyone to get hit."

The assembly did as Vegas said.

After a stunning light show, several images started to take shape out of the spiraling light. When the process was finished, all light in the room had drained away except for a bright glowing white orb the size of a basketball that appeared just above Vegas' 3D imager. Three other balls of light circled the larger orb as other lights danced around everyone in the distance. Thanks to the goggles everything else had been blackened out to the point that there was no longer any sense of depth in the office. There seemed to be no floor, walls, or ceiling. Everyone appeared to be standing in the void of space looking at endless illuminations in every direction.

"Where did everybody's goggles go?" Blu asked.

"They blend into the 3D holographic projection rendering them invisible," Vegas answered.

"What the hell are we looking at?" Rob asked, nursing his beer.

"We are standing in a 3D hologram of our galaxy. For now, I limited the hologram to our solar system. That white ball of light in the center is our sun and the three small specks of light are Mercury, Venus and Earth. Right now the projection is to scale."

"Interesting," Deep began, "Tell me, Vegas, why did you ask us to back up if this is a hologram? What did you mean about not wanting us to get hit?"

"I meant exactly what I said. This isn't a normal hologram. I constructed it out of hard light."

"Hard light?" Zo asked with a raised eyebrow. "How is such a ting possible?"

"Oh my—Vegas—did you—do what I think you did?"

"Yes Professor, I believe I did." Vegas smiled clearly proud of himself.

"Ummm, somebody wanna fill me in?" Rob started with his southern drawl, "cause it just looks like he made some fancy light show that could knock ya on ur ass and give ya a black eye if ya ain't paying attention."

Deep smiled as the astonishment struck him. "So much more than that Rob. Vegas has discovered the Higgs."

Everyone looked from Deep to Vegas, then at each other, in confusion waiting for an explanation. Vegas fought back a smile; he enjoyed their bewilderment much more than he probably should. Vegas let everyone speculate for several seconds before educating them.

"For years scientists have been trying to find what was called the Higgs or the god particle. For most of the people looking for it, it was a way to discredit religion or explain the supreme evolutionary principle. That principle has been defined as the life force, which is the impetus behind all movement. Its blind intention is to evolve and expand consciousness, life, and experiences throughout the infinity of the universe. Put plainly, a force whose objective is to know itself in a myriad of forms and circumstances.

"At its core, however, it's much simpler, yet extremely more complex. The god particle I found is nothing more than the bridge between the tangible and the intangible. It's the understanding of why matter has mass."

"Whatever da hell that means," Rob interjected. "I just want to know how da hell I'm gonna get another beer if I can't find the frig?"

"I'll get you a beer when we're done, Rob," Vegas promised.

"Wait a minute, isn't matter and mass the same thing?" Joe asked.

"No, Joseph. They are not one and the same." Deep retorted, "I believe you would know that if you had attended your classes this week."

"Sorry about that Professor Willis, but I was helping Vegas get ready to save the universe and all. That's a good enough reason for me to not be kicked out of school right?"

"I suppose. Vegas, when did you achieve this? This could be the greatest discovery in scientific history. Why haven't you shared it?"

Topaz huffed louder than necessary, and then rolled her eyes.

Vegas ignored her and answered Deep, "I can't share it. Science isn't ready. This means the collapse of the foundation of physics as we know it."

"Congratulations," Panda Jack snarled, "Now, what does this have to do with why we're here?"

Zo reached into his pocket as Panda Jack spoke, then lit up a thick five inch blunt, took a slow drag, and exhaled. "I'm wit da Panda. You'n the Prof can talk ya nerd talk some otha time. Why we be here mon?"

"Ok, to the point then," Vegas said spreading both his hands toward the white sphere representing the sun.

"Everybody gather on the opposite end of the room from me and stay back at least ten feet. If you get any closer, the hard light can hit you, and trust me, that shit hurts. The 3D imager makes the light intangible again after the ten foot limit."

Vegas used his hands, pushing in circular motions away from himself causing the light to flash and twist. The gloves on his hands allowed him to interact with and move the hologram at will. Vegas continued the hand motions until a small red light was in the center above the hologram device. He then connected both hands forming a square, and then slowly moved his hands away from each other. Simultaneously the light at the center grew until the Jovian giant was recognizable. Around the planet orbited dozens of lights, some bigger than the others—all different colors.

"All right, sorry that took me a while, but like I said this hologram is to scale. For anyone who never paid attention in grade school astronomy, this is the planet Jupiter and its over fifty-eight moons."

"Wow, Jupiter—why should we care?" Jen remarked sarcastically.

"Because, this is where we need to go to save the universe."

"Wo,wo,wo! You try'n to tell me you want me to fly with you to Jupiter? Now, you are aware that I won't even get on a damn airplane unless I'm shit-faced!" Rob stated.

Blu stepped forward. "Why the hell would we sign up to go with you to Jupiter, Vegas?"

"Because this is where Chosen One told me I had to go to save the universe. I figured that part would've been obvious."

"How would we even get there?" Deep asked with more intrigue in his voice than conjecture.

"Joe and I took care of that."

"Vegas did all the designing, but I helped with the assembly," Joe announced.

"Why Jupiter, mon? Wha be special bout that planet?" Zo asked.

"I told you it's where Chosen One told me to go."

"Why there?" Panda Jack asked. "I don't care who said what, Vegas, you ain't the type of person to do anything unless something's in it for you."

"The survival of the universe isn't good enough—really? All of you really think that bad about me?"

This time it was Topaz who stepped forward to address the group. "Stop dodging the fucking question, Vegas, what are you hiding? What's on Jupiter that's so important?"

Vegas surveyed the room and discovered the consensus of the group was to have this question answered. Vegas was hoping to save this part for last but didn't see any options now.

Vegas grunted, and then used his hands to rotate and zoom in on a section of the planet's southern hemisphere. When he found the proportions he wanted, he turned the image around to face his would-be allies.

"Any of you know what you're looking at right now?" Vegas asked.

Silence.

"Anybody?" Vegas repeated.

"Looks like a big red tornado if ya ask me," Rob alleged.

"It's Jupiter's great red spot," Deep corrected. "It's an anti-cyclonic hurricane over three times bigger than Earth. It's the biggest single storm found in the solar system and it's been raging visibly from Earth for over four hundred years."

"Thank you Professor," Vegas smiled.

"Aw damn," Blu said then motioned for Zo to pass his blunt. "I need to get high or something, I can tell this is going to be some shit."

Zo, passed the blunt. "Don't be hit'n that too rough now. That herb make purple haze look like kiddie shit."

"Save your concern, Rasta, I know how to smoke," Blu, replied taking a slow drag.

"I don't see how a giant hurricane can save anything," Jen stated. "I assume there is more to this."

"You assume correctly," Vegas confirmed with a tight smile. Vegas flipped the image of Jupiter so that the hurricane was facing upward and then motioned his hands in a way that caused the hologram to dive deep into the planet's atmosphere.

Vegas kept motioning the hologram downward as Deep asked, "Vegas, are you suggesting that you want to travel into Jupiter—at the center of the great red spot?"

"That's exactly what I'm saying. We have to travel to the planet's core in order to reach—this!" Vegas said as he finally reached the core of the 3D Jupiter model where the silhouette of a humongous structure was outlined in shadow and a reddish vortex.

"What the hell is that?" Rob asked.

"That is where we have to go. It's a temple built by the Titans," Vegas responded.

"Titans? You mean the ancient Greek myth Titans?" Topaz speculated.

"Yep, those guy."

"Wo, wo, wo! You try'n to tell me that all that ancient Greek shit ain't shit, them things are real?" Rob exclaimed.

"Yep. They're real."

"How do you know they are real?" Blu asked between puffs.

"Chosen One showed me they were real. He took my mind on a cosmic rollercoaster to the past and showed me the gods of Egypt and of Greece."

"If this is a holograph projection based on scientific data, how did you acquire the images of this temple?" Deep inquired.

"I didn't. It's not humanly possible to manufacture a probe to penetrate that far into Jupiter and transmit any information back. There's no material known to man that can withstand that kind of pressure."

"Then how do you know it's there?" Panda Jack grumbled from the corner.

"Chosen One took me there. I created this part of the hologram artificially from memory. All of you are seeing exactly what he showed me."

"In other words, what you're showing us now is something you created using CGI, which doesn't really prove the temple exists," Jen added.

Vegas moaned and rubbed his freshly shaved head with both hands in frustration. He felt like he were bogged down by a severe weight, a burden that no man should have to carry, and no one believed there was anything wrong. Vegas huffed, put his hands on his hips while the room hung wordless. There was only one more thing Vegas could show them—one more thing that might be convincing enough to any of them with half a brain.

Vegas used his hands to guide the hologram out of Jupiter's atmosphere, and when the whole planet was visible, he used his hands to shrink it until the red light representing the planet all but disappeared. Then, with several hand jesters, the room again burst into a spectrum of lights.

"Vegas. You said you created a 3D map of the Milky Way, is that correct?" Deep asked.

"That's right," Vegas answered continuing his hand movements.

"Would you mind telling me how you managed that?"

"I used the SDSS."

"Aaahhh, I see."

"UUUmmm, less nerd speak please. What's the SDSS?" Blu asked taking another drag of the blunt.

"Sloan Digital Sky Survey." Vegas deadpanned, "It's a program based out of New Mexico used to make a 3D rendering of galaxy clusters. But, they also made a 3D map of the Milky Way. I was able to get access to the data and add to it with probes I teleported into deep space."

"You said you couldn't do that," Topaz accused.

"If you were actually listening, you would know I said I couldn't send probes into Jupiter's dense atmosphere, but far off regions of the galaxy are fair game."

Vegas continued his hand movements until they stopped on a formation of dust and lights. Around the cluster of lights and gas, a bright cerulean light shot from the center at opposite ends.

"This is the last bit of proof I have. What you're looking at now is the super massive black hole at the center of our galaxy. The Chosen One told me to look here for proof and this is what I found. This is why I'm going through with the mission he gave me."

"Yoo, mon, jus look like fancy lights. What is be proof of? And, Blu stop ya chiff'n and past da herb."

Blu sniggered passing the weed, "Oh, right—my bad."

"What this proves, Zo, is that something weird is happening. You see those plumes of blue light? Well, that's an enormous amount of energy being shot out of the black hole. It's called a quasar. Quasars are among the most powerful naturally occurring phenomenon in space and they are relatively common throughout the universe."

"Then what's so special about ours?" Jen asked.

"Our galaxy shouldn't have a quasar at its center," Deep answered. "If it is there now, it means something significant has happened to cause such a drastic change."

"That's right," Vegas, confirmed, "Quasars are normally a black hole shooting out excess gas and dust because it can't absorb it all fast enough. All that gas and dust comes from the black hole being new and our super massive black hole isn't new enough to have a quasar in it, yet there it is. Chosen One told me that Gor was being reborn. I can only assume this is where his resurrection will happen."

The room got just a little more gloomy and ominous when Vegas mentioned the name Gor. When The Chosen One of Legend first arrived on Earth, he used his powers to communicate his mission to every living thing on the planet. Every man, woman and child knew exactly who and what Gor was. Gor was a force of nature unlike anything the universe has ever known: Gor is death, Gor is the omega. Chosen One had traveled to our dimension to track down the weakened Gor and stop him from being fully revived. The

Chosen One had been unable to save his own dimension—he had sworn to protect us with his life. He claimed our universe as his new home and swore not to fail, and now he needed Vegas to help keep his promise.

"I'm sure all of you understand why I called you now. This is serious, and we need to handle it. Gor is draining energy from the quasar he somehow created in our galaxy's black hole and he's using it to come back to life."

"Bohica," Rob said.

"Exactly," Vegas retorted.

"Wait, what does that mean again?" Blu asked.

"It's just a say'n for when things go from bad to worse, hun," Rob answered, "Stands for; Bend, Over, Here, It, Comes, Again. If Gor's make'n a run at life, that's as bad as it gets."

Again, silence permeated the air. Vegas was content to let everyone sit with their thoughts for a moment. Maybe they weren't all as stupid as they seemed most times. When someone finally spoke up, it was Topaz, and, of course, Vegas was disappointed.

"Wait-a-minute. How far away is that thing?"

"What thing are you talking about, Topaz?"

"The center of our universe, how far away is it from us?"

Vegas huffed already knowing where this was going and how it would end. "It's the center of our galaxy, not the universe and it's about 25,000 light years away from our solar system."

"Wo, wo, wo, heeyyyyy, wait just a minute," Rob cut in, "I don't much claim ta know about astronomy, but if something is 25,000 light years away that means it takes light from that object 25,000 years to get to us, right Vegas?"

"Yes, Rob, that's right."

"So how do we know we're not looking at a 25,000 year old quasar? Maybe we're just now able to see it."

"He's got a point," Jen insisted.

"That would be the case, but I told all of you about the probes. I was able to teleport out into space to finish the 3D map." Vegas clapped his hands and the image of the quasar disappeared, leaving behind a regular black hole.

"The day Chosen One came to me, I sent probes out to our super massive black hole and surrounding areas of the galaxy. Within five minutes of the probes being sent, this happened." Vegas snapped his fingers and the room blew up in a maelstrom of lights and colors. Vegas had shown his friends something only a handful of people would ever see—the spectacular birth of a quasar.

Another pause of silence hung in the air until the storm of light subsided and the image had returned to the quasar that Vegas had originally shown everyone.

"It will take thousands of years before people on Earth will see this Quasar, but it came out of nowhere months ago. It doesn't make sense for it to accrue naturally. The conditions just aren't right for it in our galaxy."

"Assuming we all believe you and decide to help, where does that big red temple thing come into play? What's there?" Topaz inquired.

Hands on his hips, huffing in aggravation, Vegas reluctantly answered the question, "The Chosen One told me that in the temple is a source of endless power."

"Hay! I knew it! This is all about you and your mad grasp for powers isn't it!" Topaz charged.

"This is nothing like that! I didn't even know about this thing until Chosen One showed it to me!"

"What type of power is it?"

"I'm not sure."

"How does it work?"

"I don't know."

"Of course not, and I assume you're the only one that can acquire this power, right?"

"I didn't have time to make plans for someone else to do it, plus Chosen One came to me so--"

"Bullshit! Bullshit, Vegas! This isn't the first time you've tried to play us to make yourself powerful. It's just the first time you've had the balls to actually try to pull the wool over all our eyes at the same time!"

"That's not what's happening now damnit! Chosen One came--"

"Oh, stop it! Just stop it. Do you really think that anyone here would believe for a second that the Chosen One would come to you for help! You of all people—you who tried to kill the man by draining his powers for yourself."

"It didn't exactly go down like that, but it all worked out, didn't it? Besides, why you bringing up old shit?"

"Because, that old shit is proof you're an ass and a liar. That's why I brought it up! You've proven your character time and time again unlike this fancy light show."

"What? Anyone with half a brain could come to the same conclusion if you looked at the data."

"Fuck you and fuck your data! What did you show us? A CGI shadow of a temple that probably doesn't exist and an image of a 25,000 year old ball of light and you expect us to all just fall in line behind you and do whatever you say. When were we even supposed to go on this wild trek across the stars with you, Vegas? Let me guess, we have to leave right away or we're all doomed right—right?"

"I needed time to formulate plans and work everything out. Chosen One came to me and gave me a six month deadline to get the power. We have to leave in the next several hours to—"

Topaz began clapping her hands cutting Vegas off. "Beautiful! Isn't it beautiful, ladies and gentlemen? Vegas Baby has done it again. Here was another excellent challenge for him to stroke his own ego and try to manipulate us into doing what he wants. Did you hear—we have to leave right now or we'll all gonna die. We have to tell him he's the smartest man on the fucking planet, let him lead us to our deaths and kiss his ass, or the Earth will be knocked out of its orbit and mankind will freeze—or may just explode. Oh, and we have to all get on our knees and suck his dick or the universe will be destroyed!"

"You're taking this too far, Topaz!"

"Then why didn't you tell us about this six months ago?"

"I didn't have time to! It's not my fault you're all a bunch of idiots! I need your powers not your brains."

"You don't trust anyone to do what needs to be done but yourself. You don't have any powers, Vegas, get the fuck over it."

"Bitch, you need to calm the—"

Suddenly Topaz's eyes pulsed with ferocity as she jabbed at the 3D imager in the center of the room shooting a bolt of energy that obliterated the device. With the device gone, the 3D goggles no longer worked and everyone was plunged into darkness. One-by-one Vegas' guests ripped the goggles from their eyes except for Topaz, the power in her eyes had already disintegrated the goggles—power that still burned vividly.

"If you ever call me that again, you better be prepared for an extensive stay in the hospital! Don't you dare call me outside my name again! You understand me?" Topaz spat, her hands shaking, her body filling with power that was only surpassed by her anger.

Vegas looked away from Topaz, his lips tightened while his tongue rolled in his mouth. Vegas looked down at the ground massaging his goatee, nodding to himself, and then clapped his hands together igniting a customary crackle of energy that linked his mind with the power glove.

Vegas looked up at Topaz with a raised eyebrow, his chin held high and pompous. After that he shouted as deeply and defiantly as he could, "BEY-OITCH!"

In an instant, Topaz lunged forward with murderous intent and Vegas raised his hands, the red effervescence already forming some strange menacing weapons. It all happened so quickly; only Jen had enough foresight to react.

In a flash, Jen positioned himself between Topaz and Vegas. "Enough!" Jen demanded. With a jab of his hand, Jen was able to knock Topaz back to the side of the room she came from. Next Jen turned to Vegas and with a minor focus of chi from his fingertips, he negated the energy of the power glove before the weapon could fully form.

Everyone's eyes were on Jen as he calmly back stepped to where he had stood without saying another word—as the most powerful person in the room, he didn't need to speak to get his point across.

Vegas stood and stared at Topaz. He then looked at everyone else. "You know what, fuck it! Fuck all ya'll. You don't want to help me; you can't put the past in the past then fine! I told all of you before I started the hologram that I didn't have much I could show you. I'll go in space and save all your asses my damn self! You can thank me when I get back. Now, if you aren't coming with me, get the fuck out of my place."

No one moved for several seconds. They all seemed to be scanning each other, waiting to see what the person beside them was going to do. It was Topaz who made the first move. She rose to her feet, stared Vegas down and took a slow deep breath. Wordlessly, she left the office. Her mentor Jen followed behind her.

"Anyone else leaving?" Vegas asked as the door closed behind Jen.

"You know I could a stopped you two from fighting, but—this weed hit'n pretty hard ya know." Blu giggled.

"I told ya woman, that herb--"

"Damnit Zo! You know what, you and that half-baked heifer both get the hell out. I don't need some fucking stoners following along getting me killed."

Zo closed his eyes, bowed his head and lifted both hands. Without another word he ushered Blu out of the office without looking back.

Vegas looked at the remaining people in the room. "Well?"

"I've been helping you put a ship together for the past couple of weeks. You know I'm going," Jo said grinning.

"I'm in, too," Deep announced.

Everyone turned to Rob.

"Awww, shit," Rob got up from his seat and got another beer out of the frig, then addressed Deep, "Are you sure you buy inta all this?"

"It adds up to me, yes Rob. Besides I'd rather go and find out Vegas was lying than to not go and find out he's telling the truth."

Rob looked at the ground while cradling his beer, then looked from Deep to Vegas to Jo, and finally back to Vegas.

"I don't trust you, but I trust Deep's judgment. If he's going—then Robert Holley, A.K.A Miner 49er and his powers are at your service."

"Just the four of us, all righty then," Vegas said clapping his hands, "Joe please show these two how to get to the ship. I have to revise our plans. Gentlemen, we're about to save the universe."

Chapter 4

That went well, Vegas thought. As his three volunteers left the office, Vegas allowed himself just a brief smile. Vegas was about to burst out laughing when he blinked only to find Panda Jack appearing in front of him with a rush of red smoke. The shock was enough to force Vegas to fall flat on his back.

"What the--" Vegas yelped and by reflex alone clapped his hands together, but stopped when he saw Panda Jack's antique Colt 45 revolver hovering inches from his forehead.

"Don't even think about it!" Panda barked.

Vegas lowered his hands so that his palms were facing the ceiling and let the energy in his glove fade without a weapon forming.

Panda stood over Vegas, the red fog already dissipating around him. Vegas noticed the faint smell of gunpowder, cigarette smoke, and something similar to what Vegas thought a burning forest would smell like.

"You think you're real slick don't ya, Vegas."

"What the hell are you talking—"

"Don't insult me! I've spent years watching you. I know your game."

"Why don't you throw me a bone here, Panda? What game are you talking about?"

Panda quickly pulled the hammer back on the 45. "You know what the fuck you're doing. You planned to have Joe, Deep and Rob go with you on your quest the whole time. You never intended for the rest of us to go with you."

"If you're so sure that's the case, why didn't you say something sooner?"

"Because I wanted to see how far you would go. That whole damn lightshow you put on was just to impress Deep and you were extra, extra nice to Rob. How many beers did you let him have? I remember Zolomon trying to get one of your beers and you almost shot him! You're a selfish prick who never does anything nice without a reason."

Damn he's good, Vegas reflected.

"That's not entirely true," Vegas protested. "Sometimes I play with the puppies at the local pet store and I even take toys to the kids at the orphanage just because it puts a smile on my face."

"Spare me the rants, Vegas, you don't do any of that shit."

"Maybe I do, maybe I don't. I'm not lying here, Panda. Sure I have my vices but for whatever my reasons, you have to admit I help people. I save lives—you know that."

"I know that I wouldn't trust you as far as I could throw you—cause I could throw you pretty damn far."

"If you don't trust me, then why didn't you say something before everyone left? I can't believe you'd keep quite out of curiosity alone."

"Besides wanting to see what your play was, I kept my mouth shut for one reason and one reason only."

"Which—is—?"

Panda placed a heavy boot on Vegas' chest driving his heel deep into Vegas' sternum. "Because I believe you."

"Well, thank you, Panda," Vegas said roughly, the boot pressed against his chest was making it hard to breathe let alone talk. "Why, may I ask, do you believe me? Joe is dying for some adventure, I applied to Deep's scientific mind and curiosity, and Rob would follow Deep to hell and back. What got you on board?"

"I have my own reasons."

Vegas felt Panda Jack's weight pressing down on him. If it weren't for the nannites in his system repairing his bones, his chest cavity would've been crushed. Vegas pushed out the pain and looked deep into Panda's eyes. Past the deep black patches under his eyes and withered lines representing years of pain, Vegas looked deep at Panda Jack until he thought he had his answer.

"You can feel it, can't you? You can feel Gor coming back."

Panda's eyes narrowed. "No I can't feel Gor, but I feel that something's off. That's all you need to know."

"Then if you believe me, you know I'm the only hope to save the day. Which means you won't be pulling that trigger, will ya, cowboy?"

"No, I won't. At least not now."

"Good, you want to come with us? It's a long way to Jupiter and we could use someone with your sunny personality on board."

Panda snarled, "No, I'll be staying here. Do you know why?"

"Aaaaahhh, nope, but I'm sure you'll tell me."

"Because I'm sure whatever your plan consists of, you consider Joe, Deep and Rob expendable. If you come back and they don't—I'm going to kill you."

"What? Are you serious? Do you know how dangerous the shit we're about to do is? I can't guarantee any of us will come back alive."

"Guarantee, no, but I'll be able to tell by looking at you what when down. You're an open book to me now, Vegas. If you let them die, I'll know."

"How exactly would you be able to do that?"

"I have my ways."

"You know if I come back, I'll be coming back with limitless power," Vegas said as a sinister smile edged his lips.

Panda's boot pushed down harder on Vegas' chest causing a rib to crack, and his gun was pushed tightly against Vegas' skin. Vegas grimaced as Panda leaned in close enough for Vegas to catch the smell of tobacco on Panda's breath. Then Vegas saw something he had never seen Panda Jack do before. His face seemed to morph into something that still looked like him, but somehow looked much more threatening. It was as if he were wearing some mask that wasn't completely opaque. Panda's eyes had a faint evil red glow, as if there were some kind of demon inside him that had been caged for an eternity, but was on the precipice of release. Panda's gaze penetrated Vegas on a level he had never felt before. Vegas would've said he was afraid—but that didn't seem to be strong enough a word. Vegas felt himself start to sweat and his heart pound against his cracked chest.

"I don't give a fuck what powers you come back with, you have no idea what I'm capable of. If you don't come back with those three, you and I will have words," Panda snarled in a voice not quite his own.

Then, just as suddenly as he appeared, Panda Jack teleported away in a haze of scarlet smoke. As quickly as he could move with broken ribs, Vegas raised his gloved hand into the fading smoke.

Panda might be able to read Vegas like a book, but he couldn't think five moves ahead like Vegas could. Vegas never intended to defend himself when he activated the nannites in his power glove. Instead, he turned the glove into a handheld analysis machine. The glove sucked up Panda Jack's leftover smoke and analyzed as much of it as possible. Within seconds, the glove gave Vegas a result. He checked the display where it read: SUBSTANCE UNKNOWN.

Wow, big surprise, Vegas thought. He laid on his back and let the nannites heal his cracked ribs. The pain was terrible but over quickly as the nano machines forced his ribs back into position, then healed them. Painful, but worth it. In the years he had known Panda Jack, he was never able to get that much information on his powers or personality. Vegas was sure that was the most he had heard Panda talk at one time, plus now he finally had some sense of how strong Panda was.

When Vegas was finally able to sit up and breathe normally, he got up and headed for the ship where his three helpers were waiting. As he walked, Vegas reconsidered Panda's threat. It was one that couldn't be easily dismissed. The natural question was if Panda was so powerful, then why wouldn't he do something about Gor himself? Vegas didn't know enough about Panda to feel comfortable calling his bluff. Nevertheless a smile still curled the edges of Vegas' mouth as he pondered Panda. A piece on the chest board had just made itself more interesting.

Bonus.

* * * *

Joseph Warfield was so excited he couldn't stop smiling. Next to the time Vegas took Joe to the bunny ranch and bought him two chics for his eighteenth birthday, this was the most exciting trip he had been on. Joe was about to see something that no one he knew would ever see. He was about to travel to another planet and see it up close and personal. How many people could say that shit? As Joe led Rob and Professor Willis to the ship, he realized how quiet it was, and if Joe hated anything, it was quiet.

"I'm happy you guys signed up. I thought it was gonna be just Vegas and me. Hey, Professor Willis, can I call you Deep now that we'll be working together to save the universe and all? I totally promise to still call you Professor Willis in class or if I see you in public."

"I suppose you can call me Deep for the time being, Joseph."

"Sweet! But if that's how it is, you gotta call me Joe—my mom calls me Joseph, ya know."

"Ya sure ya wanna tag along, young fella? This trip sounds more dangerous than a trip to da dentist. Ya look like ya bout ta go to a college party wit a all you can fuck hooker buffet."

"Ha! That's funny. Imma use that. But hell yeah I'm going, this is a chance of a lifetime! I'm from a small town in Oklahoma. Do you know how hard I had to work to get out of there and move to Vegas. I love my home—don't get me wrong—but nobody there is ever going to do anything with their lives. They'll grow-up, get jobs, fuck, have kids, be happy in between times when their absolutely miserable, then they'll die never seeing anything really amazing or taking any type of real risk. I don't know about you, but I'd rather die trying to do something great I believe in, instead of playing it safe until I get old and useless."

"Hmm, well said. How old are you young'n?" Rob asked.

"Just turned twenty-two my man. Hey, can I call you Miner? Your hero name is fucking awesome. Miner 49er! How you come up with that shit?"

Rob chuckled. "My father was a coal miner in West Virginia. His buddies gave him that name because of the 49er belt buckle he always wore that he passed down to me. I started wearing the thang little after he died when I was fifteen and I picked up the name somewhere along the way. I've always been called that and I've actually always hated it. Especially when I got these powers. It was like God was playing some kind of sick joke. Being called that all my life then BAM, I get powers like these. Now I figure it's just who I'm suppose ta be. So sure, call me that all ya want."

"Bitch'n! Hey Deep, can I call you by your hero tag line? Obsidian is a cool ass name too."

"I prefer that you didn't."

"What about calling you the Big O?" Joe asked.

"What?"

"You know Big O, for Obsidian. You got to admit that's a bitch'n name!"

"Let's just go with Deep for right now."

"That's cool. Just check'n. But keep that in mind, Big O."

"How far is it to Vegas' ship?"

"It's close," Joe answered. "It's down past the training room. Vegas somehow extended it adding a hanger beside his lab. All of his cars are gone, so I think he basically converted the garage, too."

Within moments the trio was entering an elevator that lead to Vegas' underground lab. The three of them had never fully understood how Vegas' lab worked, but at some point Vegas had pioneered some technology, at least so he said, that allowed him to maximize space in a structure. The inside was much, much bigger than the outside. It was like walking into a normal two-story home only to find that the inside is the size of a football stadium.

The elevator stopped at the floor-marked garage and the trio exited. Instead of the rows of vehicles that normally filled this floor, there was nothing inside but a huge spacecraft. The craft was silver and streamlined. It had no visible windows. Even the front was solid and it had two crescent wings. Three landing pads held up the ship making it ready for launch.

"What the hell is that?" Rob asked.

"That's our ship Miner." Joe answered.

"It looks like a silver bullet with a cut out styrofoam half circle wings on it! I ain't get'n in that damn thang!"

"I know it doesn't look like much from the outside, but wait till you see the inside! Trust me, it'll blow your freak'n mind, man. I tried to get Vegas to change the outside but he kept saying the simpler the better."

"Has Vegas made some changes to his facility?" Deep asked, "Somehow it looks much—bigger."

"Yeah, I think he mentioned something about expanding the surface area matrix to make room for the ship or some shit. I don't understand half of what he tells me most times, but I know he basically left the outside the same size, but made the inside bigger. How the fuck—IDK."

"Interesting. I don't understand how he does it, but I understand the basic mechanics, expanding this already large space must have been extremely difficult even for Vegas. I wonder what else he's been working on that required so much more room."

"You'll see soon enough, my friend," Vegas said walking up behind Deep and the others. "For now I need you and Rob to test out my new training facility. If it can handle you two, it can handle anything. Plus I need you two to be sharp. Who knows what'll be waiting for us up there."

"Ya regcon we'll have ta fight some old school monsters in space?" Rob asked.

"I don't know, but it's possible. I'll remotely set the training program for something that'll work for both of you. Go ahead down. Joe and I have some last minute tweaks to make to the ship and the rest of the equipment."

"Awww, Vegas, what the hell can be left? I was all jazzed to show them the ship."

"Relax, Joe, it's not like the ship's going anywhere without us. You guys go ahead and get a work out in. We need to leave in four hours, so don't go to hard on each other this time and be back here in two."

Rob began popping his knuckles. "If you're sure we can't help with anything else here, I never miss a chance ta whip the floor with the prof here."

"HAA! You and what army!" Deep replied.

"What army, ya say? Well, allow me ta reacquaint ya, my friend." Rob placed two fingers and his thumb on one of the two wristbands he always wore and twisted in a clockwise motion. Once he completed a half circle, an orb of blue energy appeared beside him. Rob reached into the energy and pulled out the weapon he used to amplify his powers—an oversized pickaxe. "Me and this army—that's who."

"Nobody is scared of that toothpick. Let's get this over with."

Rob flung the axe over his shoulder then cradled it. "Are ya sure you're all right? No normal reason I could think why a man would be in such a hurry for an ass wopp'n."

"Oh, come on." Deep laughed as he and Rob headed to the training facility leaving Vegas and Joe to whatever business they had.

* * * *

"All right, Vegas, what do we have to go over?" Joe asked excitement in his voice.

"I want you to go over the flight simulator again."

"Seriously? I helped design the ships controls. I'm nice flying the ship already."

"Yeah, but I want you to practice some combat simulations."

"Wooo, you think it'll come to that? I thought you said I was gonna be just flying there and parking the damn thing."

"And that may still be what'll go down, but I want to be sure we're prepared. With everyone else flecking out on us, we don't have near as much fire power as I hoped."

"Vegas—can I ask you something?"

Vegas looked at his friend and for the first time since he told Joe about what he was planning saw worry in his eyes.

"Yeah, what's up?"

"Why did you pick me to go with you? I mean, I'm a 5'5 white guy barely over a buck thirty with no powers. Why would you want me for something like this?"

"Are you kidding?" Vegas asked placing a reassuring hand on Joe's shoulder. "I need you because you're cool under pressure and even though you might be scared shitless, you still can manage to do what you need to do to survive and save others. I've seen you do that time and time again. Plus you're really good with machines, and you can put almost anything together if you have a blueprint even if you don't understand how it works. I never would've been able to built all this shit in time without your help— and powers? Please, I don't have any fucking powers. And just between you and me—it takes a lot more balls to do what we do without powers. Makes us better than all those bastards that were here if you ask me."

Joe smiled and nodded. Vegas felt comfortable that Joe had his confidence restored, which was good because the survival of everything may rest on his shoulders. Vegas didn't want it this way, but making a plan given all the things he knew and didn't know, there was no way to get around it. If things went south, Joe would be the one having to save the day.

"Now come in the ship. We'll triple check the equipment we're bringing to get to the planet's surface and the stuff we need to get back home. Then you can run the training program again."

"Sir, yes sir!"

****

Deep and Rob were standing in Vegas Baby's training facility and couldn't believe their eyes. They both knew they were underground, but when they opened the door to the training room, it was as if they were walking outside on a clear sunny day. Instead of a room, they had walked into a wide-open space—a desert full of boulders and canyons. The weirdest thing was that the door seemed to be suspended in reality; it was there but it wasn't. You could walk around, behind, or even jump over the door, but walking through it lead back to Vegas' lab.

"I don't even wanna know how this crap works," Rob remarked.

"Vegas certainly never ceases to amaze, does he? Always bigger and better."

"This stuff is just freaky, if ya ask me. Walk through a doorway that's underground, that leads outside, it's just—weird."

"I agree, it is a bit unsettling."

"Speaking of unsettling, do ya really think Vegas is on the up'n up here? This whole thing seems a little farfetched, even for him."

"True, but I don't think we can take the chance that he's right. I believe the others had more—personal reasons for not believing Vegas."

"Still, it makes ya think, don't it? What if us helping him makes a bigger mess than the one we're try'n to avoid?

"Vegas has seemed power hungry before, but he did present some interesting facts. Plus from the modification he's made to his lab, I can tell he's put a lot of work into this. Until I see something that tells me otherwise, I'm committed to my decision to help him."

"If that's how ya feel, then I'm with ya. Move'n on to less depressing topics, let the ass kick'n begin!"

"If you're in that much of a hurry to get a beat down, hang on let me get ready." Deep responded.

Deep began to remove his glasses and the rest of his clothes until he was down to his underwear that came midway down his thigh. He folded his clothes neatly and placed them on a nearby rock. Deep then took a heavy breathe, and his transformation began. A purple haze formed around Deep followed by a purple sizzle of energy. Deep felt his body expand as his skin grew rough and rigid into a rocky dark shade of amethyst. His height remained the same, but his arms, legs and torso grew thicker. His hands morphed until he had only two fingers and a thumb, and his feet grew wider and thicker with only two toes. His eyes were glowing a warm hue of red. When the purple energy was gone and the transformation complete, nothing that remained resembled Professor Deep Willis except the specialized underwear that expanded to fit his added bulk.

"I don't think I'll ever get tired of see'n you do that," Rob chortled. "Should I start call'n you Obsidian now?"

"Might as well, Miner," Deep thundered. His voice changed considerably when powered up. Now every word Deep spoke sounded like boulders sliding down a mountain. "Now let's see if you can back up all that smack you were talking earlier."

"Wo, wo, wo!" Rob said, "Ya gotta take off that first layer before we do anythang. Ya know that stuff can cut me—crap hurts like hell."

Deep's hero name was Obsidian for a reason. When he transformed he literally transformed into living Obsidian, a volcanic glass similar to granite. Obsidian wasn't a very strong material, which caused Deep not to be very strong when he first transformed, but the material was very sharp in its initial stage. Thanks to Deep working with Vegas, he found that the more damage he took, the harder he was hit, the harder his Obsidian form became. Vegas realized that the major difference between obsidian and other volcanic materials like diamonds was the amount of pressure they were formed in and the rate at which they cooled when reaching the surface. Deep once reached a density five times harder than diamonds which caused his strength to shoot off the charts.

"I forget about my softer sharp layer sometimes. I rarely get to keep it when I'm in a fight."

"Then allow me to do the honors," Rob said taking his pickaxe, then holding it upside down and slamming it into the ground. When the axe hit, Rob felt the vibrations reverberate from the ground to the axe, from the axe through the rest of his body. Rob felt the connection to all the rocks around him build in his bones and muscles. The pressure and strength built until Rob knew he could command any rock within a hundred yard radius with just a wave of his hand.

With a flick of his wrist, Rob flipped the axe around and swung it in Deep's direction like a baseball player aiming for the fences. The axe itself missed, but the twenty tons of rock that Rob willed up from the ground connected perfectly with Deep's right side. Rob had sent Deep flying fifty yards as easily as shooting a ball across a pool table.

Deep twisted and rolled with the blow until his outer layer was gone and he was strong enough to dig into the bedrock and stop his momentum. Just as he stopped, he spotted another five-ton boulder hurtling toward his face. Deep jabbed, shattering the boulder into pieces, only to find Rob racing towards him: axe held high ready to strike, riding on a mound of rocks literally surfing an avalanche. Again Rob swung and again connected, this time with the axe itself, only Deep was ready. Deep planted his foot and absorbed the blow, then used the added strength given to his already sapphire hard shell and drove his palm into Rob's chest pushing him through the mound of rocks he was riding.

The rocks blasted past the combatants like rolling thunder as Deep used his free hand to punch Rob square in the jaw sending him back in the direction he came. Rob rolled quickly with the mammoth punch catching his balance. Next, he extended the axe toward Deep and then pulled it back towards himself, pulling all the small rock fragments still suspended in the air behind Deep crashing down on him.

Rob was on his knees leaning on his axe massaging his jaw as Deep pushed himself free from the tonnage of earth.

They caught each other's eyes and shared a quick laugh feeling a mutual respect.

"You warmed up yet?" Rob asked.

"Almost. Were you taking it easy on me?"

"Of course. I ain't try'n ta kill ya before we save the universe."

"Ha! Kill me, as if you could."

"This isn't your days in da UFC. Thangs is different out here."

"I was a heavy weight champ in UFC before I got hurt. Besides UFC is for mixed martial arts you can apply in the real world, and my old moves have worked well on you before. Why do you bring UFC up every time?"

"Because you bring up you were a champ every time," Rob said laughing. "You ready for round two?"

"Round two—I didn't hear no bell."

The pair shared a smile as a competitive spirit passed between them. Then they launched at each other—neither holding anything back.

* * * *

"How is everything checking out Joe?" Vegas yelled from the back of the ship where all the equipment needed for the mission was stored.

"It all seems to be working smoothly, Vegas. The god particle generator is working, the energy absorbers are online, and the atmospheric generator is working well. How is your avatar holding up?"

"I'm not one hundred percent confident on that. I ran tests and everything was fine, but I'm at the point where I can't test it anymore. If I do, it'll burn out, so once this thing is on, if it goes off, it's going to stay off. I wanted to have more than one avatar just in case, but I didn't have enough time to make more 'cause it took so long to work the bugs out of this one."

"You don't have to tell me, I was there when you were trying to figure that thing out. The fact you got one up and running is blowing my mind. What about your weapons for the avatar?"

"I'll be fine there, but I can't activate them until I'm on the planet's surface. They're powered differently than my normal weapons, and the power source has a shelf-life."

"Another one and done?"

"Pretty much. How's the spacefold engine?"

"Okay from what I can tell. What about the recharge machine for it?"

"It'll work, I think we're ready. Call Rob and Deep with the prerecorded message I set up. We need to get in space soon."

"Done."

Vegas wiped away dirt and grease from his hands as he stood over a table in the hanger that outlined the plans he had revised. Joe walked up and looked at the table with Vegas, "You worried?" Joe asked.

"A little, yeah."

"Nothing else you can do now. We got all the help we're going to get."

"The help doesn't bother me. I'm good with just having Rob and Deep, I know they'll do their jobs without bitching about it."

"Then what's bothering you?"

"There's so much I don't know. I have a fraction of the information I normally do going into an operation. This is like nothing I've ever attempted before, Joe. It's a whole other level. We really don't know much about Jupiter. We don't know much about its moons if you think about it, and they're the key to my whole damn plan."

"The plan is solid considering the info we have going in. If anyone can pull this off—you can." Joe patted Vegas on the shoulder—a look of stone determination on his face. As crass and ignorant Joe could be sometimes, Vegas still saw a measure of innocence in his eye. Vegas almost envied that about Joe—almost.

Suddenly Vegas heard footsteps, and saw Deep and Rob walking towards the ship. "Is it time for us to hit the road or what?" Rob said energetically.

"Woooo!" Joe screamed after getting a good look at Rob, "What the heck happened to you? Vegas said to go easy on each other."

Rob's chest and arm were bruised and battered; he had a black eye and a busted lip but was smiling as if he just had the time of his life. Deep on the other hand looked completely fine. He had no bruises of any kind and didn't even look tired as he calmly buttoned his shirt.

"I did go easy on him," Deep said grinning in Rob's direction. "He's still conscious."

"Ha! Don't let him fool ya, little man. You shoulda seen him when he was powered up. Wasn't nothing left but dark purple pebbles and flakes when I was done wit'em. He just heals when he reverts back ta his normal self. Don't worry about me, should be completely healed in da next thirty minutes or so."

"Glad you two got a nice workout in," Vegas remarked.

"You're going to have to tell us how your new training facility works," Deep said, placing his glasses on.

"Later, we need to leave now to make sure we can hit our timetable, come on."

Vegas led the way as the others followed him into the ship. The same technology Vegas used in his lab was also used in the ship allowing the inside to be much larger than the outside should allow. If this surprised Rob or Deep, they didn't let on.

"So how is this ship gonna get us there?" Rob asked. "This thang do light speed or something?"

"No," Vegas replied, "traveling near light speed is possible, but it wouldn't work for my plans. Even though we'll be all the way at Jupiter, I have several machines that need to communicate with the ship in perfect timing to function. It takes light from the sun about forty-three minutes and fifteen seconds to reach Jupiter, so it would take us about thirty-five minutes to get there doing light speed."

"So," Rob protested, "how is that a bad thing exactly? Thirty-five minutes ain't long. I use ta drive longer than that ta get back and forth from work every day in Mcdowell County."

"The time isn't the issue, physics comes into play when dealing with high speed space travel. Once we leave a gravitational center like the Earth and travel at near light speed in space, time will move slower for us than everyone else that is still here. Thirty-five minutes at light speed will jump us into the future by several hours. That would knock my machines out of sync and kill the mission."

"I ain't gonna ask what ya talk'n bout cause I already know I won't understand it. I'm just along for the ride."

"Wait, now I'm a little curious, Vegas. If not light speed how will we get there? Any other way would take years to travel that distance."

"Well, if you must know, Deep, we're going to use something I've coined as a 'space fold engine' to get there. Put simply, I'm going to make a wormhole by harnessing a vast amount of negative energy which--"

"Wooo, Tex, ya got me at wormhole aight. I've watched enough Star Trek in my day ta know what a wormhole is. No more long-winded explanations. Let's just get this show on the road."

"I like your enthusiasm, Rob. You heard the man, Joe, fire this baby up."

Joe saluted. "Sir, yes sir!" he shouted with a wide smile on his face.

Joe ran ahead and Vegas escorted Deep and Rob to their seats at the front of the ship. When they reached the cockpit, Joe was sitting in the front seat where he was flipping switches and pressing buttons in rapid fashion as if it were second nature. Vegas put Deep in a seat several feet behind Joe on the left and Rob on the right. Vegas himself took a seat further back that sat on a raised podium above the trio.

"Initiating launch sequence," Joe said.

At that moment the platform holding the ship began to rise and a hatch in the ceiling opened. Joe pressed a button and the front hull of the ship became transparent explaining the lack of windows.

"Next stop, Jupiter," Deep said unable to hide the excitement in his voice.

The engines hummed and whirled until the ship was hovering.

"Actually, Deep," Joe started as he flipped another switch and the humming and vibrating of the ship intensified, "the next stop is Valhalla."

"Valhalla!" Rob screamed, but before he could object any further, there was a sudden jerk and the ship was launched into the stars.

Chapter 5

Joe had run the simulation of the spacefold technology over two dozen times. He could make this trip in his sleep, which was probably why he thought the trip was so boring. Within seconds, they had exited Earth's atmosphere without any violent shaking or jerking. Vegas managed this by having the ship use the Earth's own magnetic field as a sling shot, something he called magnetic pulse propulsion. Joe didn't understand a thing about how that worked, only that it made the flight much smoother than it should have been.

There was a slight burning visible as the ship reached outer space and a slight rumble as the ship exited the Earth's gravity. The ship hadn't even cleared the moon's orbit before Joe activated the space fold engines. Suddenly a massive, swirling green vortex appeared directly in front of the ship, and Joe flew into it at full speed. It only lasted seconds but felt like an eternity. The green light grew brighter and stronger; it seeped into the ship almost as if the light were becoming part of the ship, and part of everyone in it. The glow attached itself to Joe and his passengers, seemingly passing through them until they reached the other side of the abyss. When everyone was able to open their eyes, they were greeted by the planet—Jupiter in the distance.

"Holy shit! Wwwwooooo! That was like rolling down a hill on roller-skates while trip'n on acid, son! Gotdamn!"

"Hell yeah, Miner, now imagine going through that over twenty-four times in a training simulation. Not gonna lie, I threw up the first few times I did that."

"I think I might throw up actually," Deep said, looking a little purple without activating his powers.

"Hold it in, sir, we're not out of the woods yet. I still need to get us to Valhalla," Joe responded.

"Ain't Valhalla Norse god heaven or some shit? Why da heck would ya wanna take us there?"

"Not that Valhalla, Rob," Vegas said as he clicked several buttons and checked the reading on the instruments. "We're going to land on the Galilean moon Callisto. There is a large impact crater on the moon's surface that astronomers named Valhalla. That impact crater is going to be the staging area for the mission. If Joe can get us there."

"Don't let him worry you guys! I only crashed the simulation like ten times, but I know to watch for asteroids now, and compensate for the gravity from Jupiter and all these moons—we're good. Probably."

Joe flew the ship at high speed dodging and weaving in between different asteroids as he made his way to the moon Callisto. This ship generated its own gravity, which allowed Joe to flip and spiral the ship without anyone coming out of their seat.

It took him minutes of concentration, but Joe managed to get the ship to Callisto. Joe hit several switches and small devices launched from the ship landing in the huge crater illuminating it, and then he gently touched down on the moon's surface.

"Helllllloooooo, Callisto!" Joe screamed, turning to his passengers, obviously pleased with himself.

"I think imma throw up," Deep said weakly.

"Let that shit out if you're going to throw up, Deep. We have a lot to go over before we get started," Vegas said as he rose from his seat.

"I'm just ready to get out there," Rob said. "I can't believe how big that planet is. And we still far away, ain't we?"

Vegas had some device attached to his forearm that he kept peeking at while staring at the built-in monitor. "You'll get a much better look soon, Rob, trust me. Deep, you okay?"

"I'm good," Deep replied weakly.

"All right, everybody gather around me, I'm going to go over the plan and your assignments. Rob, Deep, you two pay attention and ask all the questions you have now. We're all going to be split up and on our own out there. If you're having trouble completing you mission, there isn't going to be any back up and none of us is going to get a second chance. This is all or nothing."

No one said anything. They only looked at Vegas with a sense of urgency that Vegas wanted. They all knew that the pressure was on and most importantly—there was no turning back.

Vegas stroked several keys on his wrist device, then pointed to a nearby table and it lit up with a small replica of what looked like a giant electric generator with three gadgets hovering over it to form a triangle. "All right gentlemen," Vegas grinned, addressing the others, "this is where the fun begins."

* * * *

"Step one. We have to assemble this device on the surface of Io, the moon orbiting closest to Jupiter."

"That seems simple enough," Rob remarked.

"I'm glad you think so, Rob, because you're going to be doing most of the work on this one."

"Ain't never been scared to get my hands dirty. What is it and what do ya need me to do?"

"All right, everyone, pay attention. Even though this is Rob's part, I think it's important for everyone to know what's expected of everyone else. If any one of us fails, we all die."

"But really guys—no pressure," Joe laughed.

"Just go over the plans, Vegas," Deep commented, the color just now coming back into his face.

"I don't have time to explain how this works, but basically it's a generator that's going to suck the energy from the moon's molten core and its ionosphere."

"You mean a moon has a molten core—it's volcanic?" Rob asked.

"Very volcanic. It's so active that it generates the most heat for its size than anything else in the solar system besides the sun. It's only twenty-six hundred thousand miles above Jupiter, and it's also one of only three moons in the solar system with an atmosphere, albeit a very weak one. It's so active because of something called tidal heating, which is essentially Jupiter and the other moons pulling on it.

"Thanks to the tidal heating, the moon's heat can produce an estimated one hundred million megawatts of electricity. Plus as it moves through Jupiter's massive magnetic field, it develops four-hundred thousand volts of electric current across its diameter and an electric current of over three million amperes in its ionosphere."

Rob whistled. "They shoulda named that moon Tropicana—it's got juice."

"Focus, Rob."

"Sorry, I was watch'n rerun episodes of Martian on VHS before I left."

"You watch Martian?" Vegas asked.

"Yeah."

"You still use a VCR?" Joe asked.

"Yeah, what of it?"

"Annnnd moving on—this machine is going to harness all that energy produced by Io to use in the god particle machine I brought. We're going to use the hard light to punch a hole forty thousand miles down to the planet's surface where the temple is located. Your job, Rob, is to stay on the moon and divert its lava into the machine to keep the power going, which won't be easy.

"This moon is so active that it's constantly changing. You're going to have to be in tune with most of the moon, push your powers to the limit. If you can't do this, I won't be able to get to the temple, and if your concentration slips and this machine doesn't constantly get enough power to hold the pressure back, I'll be killed instantly."

Rob paused a moment as if absorbing and processing everything Vegas had told him. It was a tremendous amount of pressure to place on him, and there was no way for Rob to know if he would be able to do any of what Vegas was asking, but his face was stern and resolute. "I swear on my daddy's grave that if I get this thing going, I'll keel over dead before it loses power."

"You're going to be out there on your own, Rob."

"We're all going to be on our own, right? I'll make it happen, cap'n."

"Once we get the thing in place, all you have to do is keep lava flowing up through the bottom of it. These three generators hovering over the machine will automatically suck up the voltage in the ionosphere producing the hard light needed, you just keep the pressure built up."

"Done." Rob nodded.

"Stage two," Vegas said as he played with the device on his wrist again then pointed at the table, "we need to install this drill on the moon, Europa."

The image of a giant drill now hovered over the table. The drill looked like it was massive, but the most distinctive features were the two large tanks on either side of it and a structure on the top of the drill.

"Europa is a little further out than Io and vastly different. Where Io is mostly volcanic, Europa is covered mostly in ice and has temperatures recorded as low as negative two hundred and sixty degrees. There's no way for us to know, but astronomers and scientists have thought for decades that Europa has underwater oceans heated by the same tidal heating that fuels Io. For our sake, I hope they're right.

"This drill is Deep's mission and our only way home. The spacefold engine we used to get here is powered by hydrogen and a form of fission; in order for it not to blow us all up, I had to use materials with a self-life that would die once we cleared the wormhole. This machine we're putting on Europe is going to recharge the fuel cells for the spacefold engine. The drill is simple to use, but it's going to be a lot of work. Since Deep is impervious to heat and cold and doesn't need to breath, eat, or rest in his Obsidian form this is all you big guy."

"Why are there two fuel cells?" Deep asked.

"I don't know what this power is I'm looking for or how it'll work when I find it. We might need to fly the ship to Gor to use the power in order to stop him. If that's the case, we'll need to get to the center of the Milky Way, and then get back home after we kick his ass."

"Hadn't considered that."

"Don't worry, Deep, I got all our bases covered. Think you can handle it?"

"Just show me how it works I'll make it happen."

"Joe's going to show you how it works I'm going to help Rob install the power source for the god particles. We need that thing storing as much reserve energy as possible. Then I'll get you set up, so I can head to the planet's surface and—"

"Wait a minute," Deep interrupted, "you're not just going to walk onto the planet's surface are you? The model you showed us of that temple was gargantuan."

"Of course not. I wouldn't be able to do anything in that temple at normal size. While Rob is keeping the way clear and you're making sure we can get back home, I'm going to be using the last invention I brought to explore the temple."

"I know I'm not gonna understand da answer, but what invention?"

Vegas turned to Rob with a mischievous grin, "How about I just show you."

Vegas motioned for his champions to follow him as he lead them to the cargo hold of the ship where he stored the device that took the longest for him to make but was arguably the most important.

In the cargo hold stood a twenty-foot tall mechanical ball with a smaller six-foot ball resting on top if it. The sphere had four rods sticking out from it, two near the top and two near the bottom, each with lights and sensors on them of different shapes and sizes.

"What da heck is that?" Rob asked.

"Scientifically it's not just one thing, but put plainly—it's my avatar. This is how I'm going to search the temple for this limitless power."

"What's it do?" Rob asked, dumbfounded.

"Well, this machine is going to generate a perfect likeness of me over one hundred feet tall. My body will stay here in the ship, but with this, I'll move around just as if I were there on the surface. I'll even have use of most of the weapons I use on Earth thanks to the new nano machines I developed.

"This puppy took me forever to get working and I haven't really had a chance to test it properly. It's also a localized magnetic generator powerful enough for me to sustain a hydrogen fusion reaction of deuterium and tritium allowing it to create a tiny sun and feed off its energy."

"Ya mean this thing is powered by da sun?"

"By 'A' sun not 'the' sun."

"Well, damn."

"Hell, Rob if you think that's something, this thing also communicates with computers back in my lab that control and distribute the energy outputs so everything works smoothly without me having to adjust to the surroundings. I had to figure out

Quantum non locality to do that! Think of it as Voodoo, but with machines. See what I had to do was get photons to--"

"Wooop, ya losing me again. Let's just move on."

Vegas clapped his hands together and took a deep breath, "Right, sorry. Joe, you prep Deep on how to work the drill Rob is about to be the first man to set foot on Io."

Chapter 6

"This some ol bullshit," Rob mumbled to himself as he stood in front of the largest most complicated piece of machinery he had ever seen, then looked up to an slight haze of an orange sky. Io's atmosphere was weak but all the sediment it threw up did create an eerie haze visible from its surface. There was something very surreal and humbling about standing where no other man had or likely ever will. The weirdest thing was that Vegas had given him no space suit or oxygen tank or anything else that is normally associated with standing in the vacuum of space. Vegas had only equipped Rob with a small rectangular device that he wore on his hip. Rob couldn't believe that this little thing was able to not only let him breathe normally, but let him stand on the moon without worrying about floating away. The gadget was labeled P.A.G. which stood for Personal Atmosphere Generator. Rob scoffed when Vegas handed it to him because it was barely bigger than the old cassette players he used to have years ago.

Without asking how it worked, Rob attached it to his belt buckle and hopped onto the moon. So here he was, standing on Io with a wife beater, blue jeans, his daddy's belt buckle, and his favorite pair of Chuck Taylors, holding a pickaxe. It just felt weird like he was standing in some video game or tricked out 3D movie, but even in his mind he wondered if the ground around him would shake and explosions of lava and gas would erupt reminding him that everything around him was all too real. Vegas had given Rob some earplugs that would let him communicate with Deep, Joe, and himself, as well as, a spray that killed his sense of smell since Io was spewing sulfur everywhere.

"Welp, let's get started."

Rob held the axe upside down, and then struck it on the ground as hard as he could. He knelt down to touch the ground with his hand trying to absorb as much of the vibrations as possible. Rob had always worn two wristbands and switched designs on them from time to time. Today one had a green and white mushroom with "1 UP" written in green letters under it which referenced his love for all things Super Mario, and the other had a skull and cross bones. When Rob's powers first manifested, he was out of control, more savage beast than man, and it was Vegas who gave him back his humanity. Vegas had developed something he put in Rob's wristbands that helped kept Rob sane and in check. As Vegas left, he tossed Rob two new wristbands that served the same purpose but would amplify his powers at least ten times—or so he said.

Again Rob didn't ask how, he simply put them on and was blown away by the results. With his first strike, Rob already had influence over one tenth of the moon! Rob raised his axe and hit the ground again extending his reach, and then he did it again, and again.

Rob may not know much about physics and quantum mechanics, but he wasn't the dullest nail in the shed. He had knowledge of tectonic plates and other principals of geology back home, but this moon was nothing like Earth. Within seconds Rob reached out with his powers and felt the moon's mantel and crust were shifting and breaking in unpredictable patterns. The geologic activity was so fast and random that it was almost impossible to predict when a volcano would go off or a large canyon would split open.

Rob remembered Vegas' words. He remembered how much of this mission was on his shoulders and what was at stake. Rob had given his word that he wouldn't fail—and he wouldn't. After slamming the ground with his axe several more times, Rob felt comfortable with the amount of influence he had over the moon, and began to mold it at his will.

First, he opened up a magma chamber one mile underneath the machine Vegas installed. He had to fight the moon to keep the chamber open as he tore a crack from the chamber topside. Next, he diverted magma from a nearby volcano into the chamber from underneath then capped it to build pressure. The moon fought him at every shift; it was as if the magma were a wild animal that had roamed free for thousands of years and was rejecting having its sovereignty stripped away.

Io's crust shook fiercely under Rob's feet, and lava rushed to his position. Then as the moon was tugged on by Jupiter's gravity, it forced the magma up before Rob was ready. Suddenly, there was a river of lava racing toward Rob from all directions. He took his axe in both hands, swung it over his head, and then hammered at the moon's crust, raising the ground under him and the machine Vegas built.

Finally, he opened a canyon that drained all the lava diverting it into the magma chamber he created earlier. As the lava reached the surface, it reacted unpredictably in Io's weak atmosphere. The way it swayed and shifted in the air reminded Rob of the lava lamp his daddy had when Rob was a kid. With his powers enhanced, Rob was able to force the molten rock to do what he wanted. When all the lava was gone, Rob lowered the platform he created to its original level. Rob's chamber was full but was losing pressure because the magma was drifting off in different directions, and the gravitational pull from the other moons, Callisto and Ganymede, was forcing the rocks together not allowing magma to flow like Rob had wanted. Rob slammed his axe into the ground then stood to his full height throwing off his beater.

"Ight now ya done pissed me off!" Rob screamed picking up his axe then hammering at the ground with all his might. Each blow twisting and shaping the moon to his purpose, Rob screamed, spat, and cursed full of anger and determination. He worked feverously, straining his muscles to the limit, and his powers were pushed farther than ever before.

Finally, Rob asserted control over the conditions, but his frustration had reached its peak. "Get up from outta there!" he barked as he hit the ground one last time forcing the magma into the machine.

When the pressure was just right, the contraption lit up like Times Square on New Year's and shot a massive beam of energy to the other machines in the ionosphere that were already channeling massive amounts of electricity. Feeling very pleased with himself, Rob reached into his pocket and put on the protective goggles Vegas had given him. He then glanced over his shoulder where the planet Jupiter jealously loomed over him, like a child having to share its favorite toy.

"That's right, mother fucka, this here moon's my bitch now!" Rob growled staring up at the planet, its pull on Io threatening to undo all of his work in seconds. He looked at the gas giant and swore again to himself that the only way that would happen was over his dead body.

* * * *

"It looks like he did it, Vegas. We're just waiting for the reserves to power up and we'll be ready to punch a hole down to the core."

"Perfect. I knew Rob would be able to do it"

"Yeah, he did it, but how long can he hold it?"

"That remains to be seen. All I know for certain is that Rob is too bullheaded to give up."

"I agree with you there."

"Help me check the suit. We need to make sure everything is lined up perfectly."

Joe went to Vegas and reviewed the diagram he had drawn up to show the position of all the sensors in the suit that were used to work the avatar. It was a solid black full body suit with wires coming from all of the major muscle groups in the body. Once everything was checked and rechecked, Vegas sat on his podium and strapped himself in.

"Are you good with how to work the recon computer?"

"Heck yeah, that's the easiest thing you've had me learn."

"Go over it with me."

"When you get to the surface you'll release some recon probes into the temple. The probes will create a map which I'll be able to use to guide you to any point of interest where this power might be. The avatar will also send back video of everything you see, so I'll be able to analysis anything you come across. Relax, Vegas, I'm good on my part here. You designed the thing like a video game for god sake. It'll be like watching you play a first person shooter something—easy shit."

"Good. Be sure to keep in touch with Rob and Deep and update them on my progress. They have a right to know how things are going."

"Done."

Vegas and Joe both turned as a light in the cockpit beeped and flashed on and off.

"We're all charged up and ready to force our way onto Jupiter's surface," Joe said.

"All right, start the process."

"Are you sure this is going to work?"

"As sure as I can be. Crank it up and let's find out."

Joe went into the cockpit and did as he was told. Indicators lit up and automatic functions were set into motion as computers moved everything into position.

"I have to start linking my mind to the avatar now. When the hurricane is drained, launch me. It should take fifteen minutes for the avatar to reach the surface. If I don't come online by that time, then it didn't work and I'm dead. If that happens, get Rob to help Deep get the space fold engine powered up so you guys can get home."

"Why did you have to tie the avatar to your life functions? Couldn't you just make it like a robot or something?"

"I could have, but we're only going to have one shot at this. I needed as many of my senses as possible. Also if there's no danger of instant death, I could get lazy or careless. It'll help me focus if I know the immediate threats I'm facing down there are real."

"If you say so," Joe said with doubt in his voice.

"Trust me, this is the best way."

"I don't know, Vegas, it just—"

"Knock it out, Joe. From this point on, our only aim is to move forward. We live and the universe lives, we die and the universe dies. No second chances, no room for mistakes. You with me, Joseph?"

"Yes, sir!"

"Then let's do it. I'll talk to you when I touch down."

Vegas pressed a button activating the symbiosis between his mind and the avatar. The chair he was in reclined until he was lying flat. The last thing Vegas felt as his mind was bonded to the avatar was the cold steel straps fasten into place. Vegas closed his eyes, and then he prayed for the opportunity to open them again.

* * * *

"Magnificent!" Deep said as he looked up at a scientific marvel.

Europa didn't have an atmosphere, so as Deep looked up, he had a clear view of Vegas' machines using god particles to their full potential. There were six lights that surrounded the edges of the great red spot that lit up bright purple, and then energy connected each of the lights. All at once the purple lights punched down around the edges of the great red spot. Suddenly, the red clouds that formed the hurricane slowly started to be sucked out of the atmosphere and into space. Stage one was complete; Rob had managed to do his part.

Deep managed to wrestle his gaze away from what Vegas was doing in space and set his mind to his task. Before he got started, he noticed something very important. Europa was cold, very cold. Even while standing on the moon's surface in his Obsidian form, Deep still felt a slight chill, which worried him. Vegas had said he was impervious to cold, but that might not have been one hundred percent accurate. While Deep was able to withstand the coldest recorded temperature of negative one hundred thirty degrees, in Antarctica. Europa's surface was twice that. Vegas had never tested Deep in prolonged cold of that intensity. Vegas must have shared Deep's concerns somewhat, because instead of his normal shorts, Vegas had made a special uniform for Deep. It was a one-piece suit that covered Deep from head to toe; it was even colored black and purple with a big purple "O" embroidered on the chest. However, even with the added protection Deep still felt a chill—definitely not good.

Deep tried to force the thoughts of freezing to death out of his mind and focus on his objective. The drill Vegas had created was incredibly simple to work but severely labor intensive. All the work for it to function was done manually because Vegas said he couldn't guarantee circuitry wouldn't lock up and freeze, leaving them stranded.

To work the drill, Deep had to take a lever and push it three hundred and sixty degrees forcing the drill to dig into the ice. Then, he had to grab another lever and push it up, and then pull it down forcing the drill deeper into the ice. It was really that simple, and it was really that hard.

The ice on Europa was much denser than the ice on Earth. Deep had no idea how long it would take him to reach the "hopefully" warm waters under the ice. The whole scenario seemed ludicrous to Deep that he was about to put so much work into something that gave no warranty that he would find what he needed. Europa, being heated by the same tidal heating as Io, was something that nobody had ever been able to confirm, but their survival depended on it.

It didn't seem like Vegas to leave so much to such an unknown variable. In the past Vegas' plans had always been so well thought out. In addition, his machines and weapons always had an elegance and slickness to their design that Deep admired. Everything Vegas had brought seemed—rushed. Was Vegas forced on this path because no one else signed up? Did Vegas really not have any other options? Was he really planning to get anyone home besides himself? The more Deep slowed down and thought about everything, the more awkward Vegas' plan felt.

Again, Deep tried to focus on what he had to do. He didn't have any other choice now—he was committed. Gingerly Deep began his first rotation around the drill which took much longer than he would've thought; then, he raised the drill with the other lever and forced it down into the ice. Deep stopped to check the impact and saw he penetrated the ice less than six inches—six inches.

In the initial stage of his transformation Deep could lift over forty tons, but he couldn't drive the drill even a foot at a time. Vegas knew Deep's strength level; he also had to know the water on this moon could be miles down. For Deep's hard work to matter, he had to get to the water and get at least one of the fuel cells back on the ship before Vegas found the power he was looking for.

At that moment, Deep peered into space again and saw what looked like a comet coming from off in the distance. The comet flew into the center of the large void that used to be the great red spot and Deep realized it had to be Vegas. He also saw the effects the hard light was having on the planet. Jupiter was a planet of chaotic winds and storms, but it always looked uniform and organized as if there was a method to its madness. Now that its biggest storm had been stopped by force, the planet's red and white atmosphere stopped flowing in parallel bands. The whole planet looked angry as if sensing that it was out of balance or under attack. The colors and storm collided, twisting and distorting, until it looked like the planet was attacking the hard light.

Deep tried to wrap his mind around the amount of pressure the hard light had to be under; he tried to imagine the amount of power needed to not only get the process started but also to sustain it. Deep contemplated all this as he rotated the drill again then reached to raise the drill sighing, "I'll bet Vegas gave Rob the easy job."

Chapter 7

When Vegas awoke, he was naked, kneeling as if he were before some regal king. His eyes struggled to adjust to the awesome glow all round him like he was standing in a desert of light. His ears caught a constant rumbling and whistling of four hundred mile an hour winds off in the far distance. The ground looked like some type of blue metal that was warm and pulsing like a heart beat. Vegas used his mind to access the computer functions of the avatar to analyze the metal and found that it was metallic hydrogen.

Vegas tested his muscles, stretched his arms, clenched his fist, and then surveyed his surroundings. The temple was still huge—but not as imposing since Vegas himself now stood one hundred feet tall—but Vegas was expecting it to be bigger since he didn't get a good look at it when Chosen One brought him here. It was in the center of a hurricane that was three times the size of Earth; however, the temple itself seemed to be possibly the same scale as Olympus Mons on Mars at roughly sixteen miles high and three hundred forty-one miles across.

"Dude! Why the fuck are you naked?" Vegas heard Joe scream in his ear.

"I haven't uploaded my clothes and weapons yet, relax."

"No, I will not calm down. I have seen your Johnson way too many times man. Just cause you're hung like a bull doesn't mean you should show it off all the time—that's gay man. That's gay."

"Stop walking in on me when I have women over."

"Just get your clothes on."

Vegas closed his eyes and concentrated on the uniform stored in the avatar's hard drive. He imagined his shirt first, solid black except for a red "V" that ran down from his shoulder to his bellybutton. The left sleeve was cut away displaying his arm while the right sleeve ran down to his wrist and had a red tribal design on it. His right hand was bare, but his left was sporting his patented glove. Vegas' battle outfit was topped with plain solid black pants and a pair of red and black Air Maxes with red soles. When he opened his eyes, he was wearing everything he had imagined.

"Better?" Vegas asked.

"Much. It looks like everything is online perfectly here. Just got to check your weapons and then you're good to head in. I hope this works because going near that thing with no weapons does not sound like a fun option."

"It'll work. I'm going to summon each weapon I can then run off the number of times I can use them."

"There's a limit?"

"Unfortunately. I couldn't make them work like on Earth where they run off my own adrenaline and lactic acids, because this avatar doesn't produce any of that. The robots have a shelf-life and a limited amount of ammunition."

"So what are you gonna do if you run out of bullets?"

Vegas brushed his hands together forming his first weapon, a perfectly balanced titanium broadsword with a wide guard, that would make Conan proud. "Guns are going to have a limited use for me here. I'm mostly going to be taking an up close and personal approach when possible."

"Do you even know how to use that? I can count on one hand how many times I've seen you use any type of sword."

"Just cause you ain't seen it, doesn't mean I can't do it."

"If you say so. I'd rather have a gun or a bazooka or something."

"That's 'cause you're a pussy."

"Against some of the people I've seen you fight, hell yeah! Now how does this work?"

"I test each weapon and tell you how many times I can pull it out of the air and you keep track."

"Well, get started. I don't have all day."

Instead of arguing, Vegas proceeded to go through his arsenal one at a time.

*Titanium broadsword he could now summon 10 more times

*Titanium daggers he could use 20 times

*Titanium shield that had the letters VB embroidered on it, with razor sharp edges he could use 50 times

*A pair of 45 Cal handguns that fired reinforced steel bulletsand was the only guns with infinite ammo he could use 50 times

*A six-shooter 500 Magnum revolver firing Titanium bullets he could use 10 times

*AA-12 Shotgun that fired incendiary rounds he could use 7 times

*Dillion Aero Gatling gun firing titanium bullets he could use 5 times

*M32 Grenade launcher fires 6 rounds custom made to fires shells as powerful as an atomic explosion he could use 5 times

*Matador rocket launcher more powerful than 5 atomic bombs he could use 3 times

"Is that it?" Joe asked when Vegas was finished with the list.

"Not quite, hang on." Vegas brushed his hands together letting the energy form, touched the small of his back with his gloved hand, then touched between his shoulder blades. Within seconds, a retractable bow formed along with a quiver full of arrows.

"Are you kidding me?" Joe screamed. "A bow and arrows! You brought a useless bow and mother fuck'n arrows? What happened to all those futuristic high tech weapons you pull out all the time?"

"No weapon is useless unless you're too stupid to realize its potential. It was hard enough getting these modified nannites to work let alone having them form complex weaponry. Simpler is better," Vegas said reaching for the small of his back. The retractable bow fit neatly on his belt when not in use, but when he touched it with his glove—it would extend to its full size. Vegas extended it to check the weight and then pulled an arrow out of his quiver. He loaded the bow and pulled back to familiarize himself with the tension.

"I have twenty arrows in all. Five of which are loaded down with tons of liquid nitrogen that should freeze or at least slowdown any living thing and five arrows that will go off with a force between ten and twenty hydrogen bombs."

"Damn! What do the other ten do?"

"Those are my wildcards." Vegas slowly released the tension in the arrow and placed it back in his quiver, then hooked the bow back on his belt, "Plus, I have two other surprises that I can pull out if things get really bad. Not entirely sure I can survive them but we'll cross that bridge when we come to it. Trust me, if this isn't enough to do the job, then the job was never going to get done."

"All right," Joe said nervously, "how are you managing explosions that big though? Where did you get all the uranium?"

"Not using any uranium. I found a way for these new nano machines to create antimatter. An antimatter weapon wouldn't work at normal size because you couldn't get enough of it into a bullet to be effective, but at this size and scale in the avatar, it's the best way to pack a serious punch. I just put more antimatter in some projectiles than others. It was actually pretty challenging to create the right combination of electrical and magnetic fields to keep them contained. I had to create a vacuum to work in to avoid matter and antimatter from colliding long enough to create the magnetic casings. Antimatter is the most explosive substance in the universe and I'll admit—I almost blew myself up a couple of times."

"I was about to ask you what antimatter was when I remembered how much I don't actually care."

"It's really easy, antimatter is just—"

"Nope, don't care, just tell me what's next."

Vegas sighed. "Next, I go inside after I get the physics right."

"What are you doing with physics now?"

"I need to make sure I can move normally, as if I were on Earth," Vegas began as he jumped and flipped. "I don't want to be hanging in the air longer than normal—could cause me to make mistakes."

"You done tumbling yet?" Joe asked amused.

Vegas ignored him and calibrated his landing and movements the way he felt most comfortable with. One of the things that worried Vegas the most was gravity of Jupiter's core. The only solution Vegas could think of was to employ the same anti-gravity method he used in his shoes on Earth—thankfully it was paying off. The same technology was used on

Vegas' weapons allowing him to hold his sword, shoot bullets or missiles and use everything else in his arsenal without them falling instantly to the ground under Jupiter's massive gravity. Vegas was able to move just as freely as if he was standing in the Nevada desert. Vegas then tested his anti gravitational shoes that didn't quite let him fly, but rather stand, walk, and run on air. When he was satisfied, Vegas sprinted to the front of the temple. As he got closer, the ground morphed from its shining metallic blue into flat stone and dirt.

"Ok Joe, it's game time now. I'm going in and I have no idea what's waiting for me and I have no idea what I'm even looking for. I need you serious and focused."

"I'm with you."

Vegas felt a little better as Joe's tone changed. Just as Vegas reached what looked like a giant opening in the temple, the proximity warning went off in the avatar.

"Vegas, above you! Back off!" Joe screamed with urgency.

Vegas slid to a stop, planted both feet on the ground, and hurtled back with all his might landing on his hands, then pushed off again as a massive object came slamming into the ground where he stood seconds earlier. Vegas was still in the air when the force of the object impacting the ground knocked him almost a mile back. Vegas quickly stopped his momentum and righted himself.

"Oh, shit! What is that thing?"

"What does it look like?" Vegas asked, not able to see through the debris and dust in the air.

"Hang on. I'm running it through the recognition program—it's not coming up with an ID. I've—I've never seen anything like it, and I've seen some fucked up shit before."

Vegas was about to ask Joe to describe it when he saw three pair of blood red eyes shining through the dust. Vegas stood and positioned himself in a fighting stance, waiting to summon a weapon until he knew what he was dealing with. One pair of the eyes moved back and forth as though restless or indecisive as to what angle it wanted to attack from. The other eyes were transfixed on Vegas.

"Joe, I need to know what this is."

"I'm working on it, I'm working on it!"

Suddenly, a large beast leaped from the dust and growled like some mix between a lion and a dinosaur. The beast's roar was so loud and powerful, it almost knocked Vegas off balance. Vegas felt his body vibrate and felt fear embed itself in his spine. His heart was racing out of control as he recognized the beast. Vegas started to wonder if linking the avatar to his life functions was a good idea; meanwhile, the beast dashed towards him. As it dashed incredibly fast towards him, Vegas saw the large mighty head of a lion with huge imposing horns and a goat head where its mane should have been. Replacing its tail was a snake with the biggest head and the sharpest, most venomous looking fangs Vegas had ever seen.

"What the fuck is that?" Joe shrieked.

As the three-headed beast charged shaking the ground with every step, Vegas calmly brushed his hands together producing his shield bracing himself for attack.

"That," Vegas started, a smile formed on his face as the thrill of the challenge overtook the fear of death, "that would be a Chimera."

Chapter 8

In an instant, the massive lion's claw swiped at Vegas' shield forcing him off balance. Then the lion head seemed to swap places with the goat and tried to ram Vegas in the chest. Vegas managed to leap over the goat's horns only to meet with the snakehead that formed the beast's tail. The strike from the snake looked as deadly as it was quick, but Vegas had planned ahead and already had the shield in position to stop the snake as he flipped.

Before Vegas could land, the goat's head tried to ram him again. Vegas caught the blow with his shield and then placed his foot on the goat's head removing the shield which gave the snake an opening. The snake struck at Vegas, its fangs razor sharp and dripping acid. Vegas had opened himself up for the strike to deliver one of his own. As the snake lunged, Vegas summoned one of his daggers and the snake bit down on it just inches away from Vegas' neck. As the snake bit down on the dagger, Vegas threw the shield at the base of the three-headed beast's tail.

Before the shield could find its mark, the lion rolled saving its tail. But, not before Vegas could release the dagger to grab the snake just below its massive head. When the beast rolled, Vegas activated his shoes allowing him to stand on air which confused his opponent long enough for Vegas to use his other dagger to sever the snake's head. Vegas quickly back flipped as the great monster roared with a sound of pain and fury unequal to anything a natural lion could manage.

Vegas allowed himself to land on the ground then sprinted to his shield because the Chimera wasn't advancing on him. Instead, it was howling and barking, leaping in circles and pounding the ground with its paws. What was left of the snake was spinning in every direction, venom spewing from it like water out of a garden hoses. Suddenly, the monster's tail disappeared into a green miasma and the lion set its feet and locked its eyes on Vegas.

The beast growled so strongly that Vegas felt vibrations in the ground. Every inch of it screamed redemption, its only desire to rip, tear, slash, and claw its enemy to dust. Vegas could feel the desire to kill directed towards him and he confronted the beast staying relaxed and lowering his shield. Vegas then extended the head of the snake still clutched in his hand, dropped it to the ground and watched it turn to vapor.

"It doesn't matter how bad you want to kill me," Vegas said arrogantly, "because you can't."

Vegas had no idea if the beast could understand his words; however, his body language and tone was enough to solicit the response he wanted. Vegas' supercilious bravado got the beast to charge but while jumping in the air, it did something unexpected and spat a hefty sized fireball in his direction. Vegas blocked the fireball with his shield and swapped it away in one fluid motion only to find a claw barreling down on him. Instead of retreating, Vegas sprung forward under the beast using the shield to take a deep slice out of its stomach. With lightning reflexes, Vegas used his shoes to change his inertia while in the air until he was on the monster's back. With his remaining dagger, Vegas stabbed at the monster's spine. Once more, the monster shrieked in pain, it turned on its side scratching and clawing doing everything it could to reach Vegas, but he had already used his shoes to float above the monster.

Vegas threw his shield with everything he had, performing an instant castration on the great beast. Vegas let himself fall in front of the monster's two remaining heads, at the same moment he slid his hands together producing a .45 Cal handgun in each hand. Before the beast could attempt to get up, Vegas unloaded one clip into each remaining head.

Vegas was prepared to empty another set of bullets into the beast, when he saw that its capitulation was complete as it disappeared into nothingness. He waited, guns trained in the spot where the Chimera had dissolved, expecting some trick. After thirty seconds, Vegas was satisfied that he had killed, or at least, defeated the creature. Vegas rose to his feet and dispersed his weapons until he needed them again.

"Joe, you get all that?"

"Hell yeah, I saw that! You kicked that ancient ugly mother fucker's ass!"

"Yeah, I know. It bothers me how easy that was."

"You make shit look easy when *you* the shit. I couldn't think of five people that could do what you just did."

"I could."

"Who?"

"Not important. We're burning time. I need to make a decision."

"About?"

"About which way I should move forward. I see an entrance about nine hundred yards up, but I also could go through the front."

"Use the entrance up top. They have to be expecting that if anyone could get in, they'd be coming through the front door, right?"

"That's what I was thinking," Vegas said as he sprinted towards the temple, his anti-grav shoes already lifting him to the opening.

* * * *

When Vegas reached the opening on the side of the temple, it was completely dark inside just as he anticipated. He stood on the edge of the opening, his hands hovering in front of him ready to conjure any weapon he needed. He closed his eyes before entering the darkness and extended his other senses. He listened for any movement, tried to feel any shift in the air inside, tried catching the smell of anything on the inside, and then only when he was satisfied he was alone, he slid his hands together invoking a pair of night vision glasses.

The glasses Vegas made were similar to the ones he sometimes used back home, sleek and stylish like regular sunglasses, but allowing him perfect night vision without the bogged down feeling of goggles. When Vegas put on the glasses, he was amazed at what he saw. The opening was the entrance to a room that Vegas could only describe as a dungeon.

The dungeon was massive. There were pillars scattered throughout the room, but Vegas couldn't see where they connected to the ceiling. The darkness extended in almost every direction so that only the floor was visible. Vegas cautiously entered the room walking on air to avoid making a sound.

Vegas reached for his belt, and then unlocked the container holding all the recon probes he brought. With a flick of his wrist, hundreds of thousands of probes were released into the air. They all zoomed in different directions, some even going out the way Vegas had come in to provide information of what was happening outside the temple.

"Joe, you picking up the probes' signals?" Vegas whispered.

"Picking them up fine, Vegas. They're moving in all directions at the speed of sound, but it's going to take a few for them to get all the information possible."

"The probes will search out all points of interest and provide us with a map of the areas they traveled through. Hopefully, one of them will find whatever power I'm supposed to be looking for, but let's focus on the probes still in the room with me for now."

"Hang on. Well, from what I can see, you don't want to go up right now. They still haven't reached the top of those pillars, but the floor is maybe ten hundred yards below you."

"Down it is. Anything interesting down there? Any way out?" Vegas said as he commanded his shoes to lower him to the ground.

"Not really. There does seem to be something resembling a door way, but there's something blocking it."

"Living?"

"I'm not sure, wait a sec—I'm not picking up anything on thermal, so I don't think it's alive."

"We're dealing with mythical creatures here that turn to dust when they die. No telling if they give off heat or not."

"True."

"How big is it?"

"Bigger than the last thing you fought, that's for sure. I'm putting a marker on the map of what we have plotted so far. You should see the exit and whatever is blocking it is highlighted."

"Beautiful, I'm going silent for the next few minutes. Talk to me when you have some info, but keep quiet otherwise," Vegas murmured, his heart racing faster as he approached ground level.

The closer he got to the floor, the louder he heard a rumble, as if the stone pillars were being shaken and the air was being pushed back and forth. Anticipation built the lower Vegas traveled in the dungeon, as well as, the smell. The only thing he could liken the smell to was something like a wet dog, but much more pungent. The smell was saturating the air to the point where breathing, even though the simulated avatar, was difficult.

Following the markers placed in his glasses, Vegas finally saw the source of the odor, which was also the source of the cycling air and vibrating walls. Vegas had walked directly above the giant sleeping three-headed dog. *What the hell, is everything in this place gonna have three heads!* Vegas thought as he stood above the dog. It was lucky that he approached from the air; if he hadn't, at least one of the dog's three noses would've picked up his scent for sure.

Vegas paused for a moment to figure out how best to tackle this problem. He could see the exit clearly as well as the virtual map the probes were creating of the room and its surroundings, but they weren't giving Vegas any other option than to enter through the door that the oversized mutt was guarding. Some of the probes had gotten through the cracks at the other side of the exit, and Vegas could see the map expanding in that direction as well as the power levels spiking. Vegas was as certain as he could be that he had to get through this door, but how?

Then, it hit him.

As quickly and as quietly as Vegas could manage, he customized his glove and the nannites to produce three tactical nukes, which he outfitted with the same anti-grav tech he used in his shoes. When he was finished approximating the distance he wanted the bombs to float, Vegas let them go. His aim was a little off, but he managed to get the charges to hover a few feet above each of the dog's heads.

When he was satisfied with the placements, Vegas willed his shoes to carry him into the air. As Vegas gained altitude, he also sought refuge behind several of the stone columns in the large dungeon. He paused in the air, then took out his Matador rocket launcher, and aimed it at the center head of the dog that he had tagged with his glasses. Vegas ran the calculations in his head, thinking this may be overkill, but then he figured that it would be better to use too much than too little.

Vegas had the rocket launcher locked, then fired. The force from the rockets release shot him into the air another twenty feet, and then Vegas dissolved the rocket launcher and continued his assent. Within seconds, the rocket connected with its target causing a massive explosion. The sound rang out louder than anything Vegas had ever heard and seemed to shake the entire temple.

Cerberus, Vegas thought suddenly, *I thought a big three-headed dog seemed familiar. That must have been Cerberus. Guardian of the gates of Hades. Shit! I hope fire works on the bastard.*

The fire from the blast was still raging as Vegas lowered himself still protected from the shockwave by the pillar. As he lowered himself, Vegas looked at the other pillars, and while they had all been shaken surprisingly, none of them had collapsed. Vegas checked the readings on his glasses and didn't find any sign of Cerberus. Vegas checked the radiation readings, and then made several adjustments to make sure his avatar could handle the radiation without transferring any effect to his real body. Vegas knew the avatar could only handle so much, so he brushed his hands together then placed his left hand on his forehead.

A red glow encircled Vegas giving the avatar added protection as he sprinted though the exit. As he came out the other side of the exit, no three-headed dog in sight, Vegas couldn't help but smile to himself.

This might be easier than I thought.

* * * *

Joe sat in front of a multitude of computer screens and lights monitoring Vegas and his accomplishments. Vegas had fought his way through evil Satyrs, zombie Roman soldiers, some creatures that could turn people to stone with a look, something that looked like an Egyptian Sphinx, plus several other monsters that they couldn't identify, but nothing came as close as killing Vegas as the beautiful sirens that almost had Vegas ready to cut off his own dick and slit his throat. Not only, were there foes to defeat, but there were tons of traps—each one nearly killing Vegas, no matter how careful he was. It had been hours, but Vegas had explored less than one fourth of the temple.

Vegas had currently muted Joe from his earpiece, so he could concentrate on fighting the legion of Centaurs and Cyclops that ambushed him out of thin air. Watching Vegas fight his way through this temple was like watching someone play God of War on steroids. Unlike a video game, there were no power up or recharges to exploit. Even though he had only been through such a small portion of the temple, he had been forced to use over half of his weapons.

Joe kept monitoring the battle using the probes in the room with Vegas to let him know when he was being attacked from behind or when something was coming at him beyond his line of sight. Since the computers did most of the hard work there, Joe decided to update Miner and Obsidian on what Vegas was doing—which seems to have been a mistake.

"Well, I'm happy Vegas is have'n such a fun time with his part! Congratulations!" Rob screamed sarcastically in Joe's ear, "If it's so easy for'em, tell'em ta hurry the fuck up!"

"I never said it was easy," Joe corrected. "I said he was making it look easy. Don't go all postal on me, Miner, Vegas just thought you guys deserved to know about his progress."

"Don't worry about Rob," Deep added. "He's having a difficult time keeping Io under control."

"You damn right, I'm having a hard time. That damn giant gas mutha fucker is really pissing me off! Every time I pull, it pulls twice as hard like this is some fucking competition or some'n! And don't get me started on the other two moons, those fuckers keep shifting positions, so I never know where they're gonna tug from. What's taking so fuck'n long?"

"Calm down, Rob," Deep insisted. "Joe had told us what is taking so long. We knew when we signed up. This wasn't going to be easy."

Rob's only response was a slow agitated grunt.

"Look, Vegas and I both know you two are having a hard time, but believe me we're working as fast as we can here. Hell, the first two things Vegas ran into were a Chimera and Cerberus for cry'n out loud."

"Wait a minute," Rob started sounding much calmer, "those two are connected somehow. They got something in common."

"Yeah, they both had three heads and turned into dust when killed."

"No something else, something important."

"Are you sure about that, Miner?"

"Hey, just cause I ain't as smart as fuck'n egghead Vegas or Deep, doesn't mean I'm stupid. I got Bachelor's in Science. I could teacher high school classes and would be if it paid any damn thing. If there's one thing I know, it's my Greek myths. I was big inta that stuff when I was a kid. I just can't remember right off what the connection between those two is, but I think there was another lion or some'n, too."

"I believe Rob is right, Joe. I never studied Greek mythology very extensively, but I do recall some connections as well. Is there a way for you to look it up on the ship computers?"

"No, sir. We are way outside any type of internet connection and all the ship's systems are on keeping the ship undetected, keeping me alive, helping Vegas map his way through that temple. I got nothing left."

"I'll remember sooner or later, but I gotta go. That fat gas bitch wants to wrestle some more."

"I also need focus. I'm maybe one hundred yards into the ice, but I have a lot more distance to cover."

"All right. I'll be in touch with you both. It looks like Vegas is down to the last centaur anyway," Joe said as he pressed a button on the dash cutting off the three-way connection devoting his full attention to Vegas. Just one last enemy to defeat, then deeper and deeper into the bowels of hell—yyyaaaahhhhhoooooo!!!!

* * * *

Vegas was embarrassed by how long it took him to figure it out, but he finally knew why all these monsters kept coming back to life after he slaughtered them. Vegas had spent thirty minutes killing off Cyclopes, Centaurs and undead Roman soldiers, before realizing the power was all emanating from the largest Centaur in the room. This Centaur was at least twice the size of the others, wearing a silver armor that covered most of his body, and wielded a large spear. His torso and face may have been human, but his eyes were as full of hate and bloodlust as any demon. Its skin would shine in the light like some glossy gray rock, and there seemed to be some type of invisible power surrounding him like burning ozone.

Vegas had set off explosions removing all of the Centaur's help until it was just the two of them standing in blood and violet clumps of smoke. The gas and vapors of the fallen enemies began to reform. Seeing his chance to end the battle, Vegas used his pair of daggers to charge his adversary, yelling a war cry at the top of his lungs. Vegas used his shoes to lift him from the ground, and as the half horse-half man lifted on its hind legs to meet him, Vegas instantly dove to the ground under the monster—to the only spot not covered with thick battle armor. With both daggers, Vegas gutted the Centaur releasing its black pungent blood to the air, and then dashed and walked on air to the human half, then slit its throat.

The horse half of the monster began to wobble weakly then fell to the ground slipping in its own blood. The Centaur twitched and strained, trying to hold on to every ounce of life. It looked like it might heal itself, too, until Vegas walked over, brushed his hands together causing his left hand to hum with power, and then crushed its head with one powerful punch.

The Centaur bursted into light and dust then faded to nothingness. All the dust and coalescing enemies centered around the dead general Centaur, creating a vortex that cracked and shot lightning until it dissolved into nothingness. When he was satisfied he was alone, Vegas finally let down his guard and collapsed onto the floor breathing heavily. Even though his body was made of hard light the avatar still showed the scars of battle all over his body. His clothes were torn, whelps and bruises covered his arms and torso, and virtual blood leaked from his wounds that hurt—a lot. Vegas reached up to his ear and clicked on his earpiece so he could hear Joe.

"Vegas? Vegas, are you all right?"

"Please tell me the room is clear."

"Hang on—yeah, you're clear."

Vegas sighed deeply then completely relaxed feeling the tension of battle drain away.

"Damn, V you kicked ass in there! When you pulled out that one Cyclopes' eye then started beating those soldiers with it—damn man, I almost shitted myself," Joe said laughing.

Vegas chuckled. "Ya liked that, huh? I just felt inspired for some reason. How are Rob and Deep doing?"

"Miner is starting to feel the pressure; it's getting harder for him to hold everything together and Deep isn't making a lot of progress with the drill. He's been going at it nonstop though."

"I figured. Deep will get his part done, but I'm worried about Rob. He has the hard job—I'm not sure how much longer he can hold out on Io. I wish I had an easier way to power the god particles, but I couldn't find an alternative."

"He knows that, but it doesn't stop him from being pissed about it. I think he's cursed out Jupiter at least ten times since he got that thing going."

"How's my body on the ship?"

"Fucked up. I thought you would heal like normal."

"For the avatar to work, I had to eliminate all the nannites in my bloodstream. I need for you to get the capsules near my body labeled E.C.M. In them should be some clear powder, take that out and rub it into my wounds."

"Got it, give me a sec—I have a question by the way."

"Yeah?"

"How are you hurt if you're not there?"

"My mind is linked to the avatar and the mind is a very powerful thing. If the mind is damaged there's nothing to stop the body from thinking it is, too. It also involves the whole process of linking the physic to let me move here as I would on Earth. Like I said, if I die here, I die there."

"Oh my God, V what the hell is this E.C.M. shit? It smells like—like pure shit man!"

"E.C.M. stands for extra cellular matrix. I was experimenting with different things and found a way to make a powerful healing powder out of pig bladder."

"You mean you got me rubbing you down with ground-up pig guts?"

"Yep."

"This some nasty, funky, evil genius, psycho shit, Vegas. How the hell do you come up with this stuff?"

"Just pour it in the wounds, Joe," Vegas said pulling himself off the floor, "I'm heading in the next room. The scans showed there was something big through here."

"Shouldn't you wait until you heal first?"

"It'll start working instantly as soon as you apply it. There are only a few vials of that stuff on board and I want to save some for Rob and Deep in case they need it later."

"This shit stinks."

"Just do it."

"I am—just say'n goddamn!"

Vegas ignored Joe and continued to the room he was heading for, before he was ambushed. The probes had found a huge room similar to the one where Vegas killed Cerberus, only this one had massive amounts of gold, silver, diamonds and other precious metal. A room that ornate either had to be important, or lead to somewhere important. Before entering the room, Vegas did a quick body check. While his clothes were still badly torn, his body had almost completely healed.

Feeling ready and as confident as he could when about to face the unknown, Vegas kicked down the door. He made his way to the space marked on his glasses, but was hit with a beam of light before he could take three steps. His glasses adjusted to the light allowing Vegas to see and revealed the grandeur of the room. What Vegas saw inside was so amazing it took his breath away.

Chapter 9

As Vegas stood and marveled at his surroundings, he couldn't help feel as though there had never been, nor will there ever be, a room as lavish as this one. There were mounds of gold; rubies and other jewels stacked two hundred feet high. Gold and bronze statues of the Titans, each standing over five hundred feet tall were labeled with the name of who they were made to represent. There were statues of the Titans: Hyperion, Themis, Prometheus, and Atlas among others, but standing just a little higher than the rest, were the Titans Kronus and Gaea.

Vegas had never seen such a sumptuous collection of riches. He couldn't think of anything found in history that could compare to what he was now seeing. There was a pristine fountain that tapered off into two streams on either side of a boardwalk, its water as clear and smelled as sweet as any ocean. The ceiling and walls were covered in mosaics made of diamonds and other precious gems depicting different battles and victories of the Titans.

As Vegas continued to explore the chamber of treasures, he was hit with different fragrances that gave him an unusually euphoric mirth and enticed by sounds of waterfalls and waves that made him much too calm to be in a place so dangerous. Vegas knew in his rational mind he needed to focus on his mission. He knew he needed to find the exit to this chamber or uncover the power located here, but the ambiance had gripped his emotions like nothing he ever felt before.

"Vegas are you all right?" Joe asked. "I'm looking at you on the probes and you got this gay ass look on your face."

"Yeah, I'm good."

"Wow, you're talking in a really gay ass voice right now too—what the hell, man?"

Vegas listened to Joe's voice, he focused on it, using Joe to pull himself back to reality long enough to think straight.

"Joe, listen to me. I need you to use more of the E.C.M on me. Blow—force it up my nose."

"You sure about that, what's going on?"

"Just do it! Hurry!"

Joe's voice disappeared from the earpiece and Vegas felt himself slip into a state of total nirvana. There was no reason to leave this room; if there was a heaven, it couldn't possibly be better than this. Suddenly dozens of beautiful women began appearing from behind the stacks of treasure. Each was unique, some Black, Asian, White, every nationality of Earth was represented. Each woman was scantily clad or fully naked, and every one of them approached Vegas with a lust in their eyes. At that moment, everything drained away from Vegas. He had no cares, no ties to anything outside this room.

Then as suddenly as they appeared, they all vanished. Vegas' mind was clear and his surroundings changed drastically. The treasures, pristine waterfalls and fountains, the statues and mosaics, all vanished like the women Vegas had seen. Instead of the opulence he had just seen, Vegas was looking at a room almost identical to the one where he killed Cerberus only the pillars were spread much farther apart and the room smelled twice as bad.

"Vegas, you okay? Did it work?" Joe asked, his voice full of concern.

Before Vegas could answer, his vision continued to clear until he was able to see something massive in front of him. Vegas touched the rim on his glasses and as he adjusted them, stepped back in shock at what lay in front of him.

Vegas stood before the largest, most majestic, and noble looking lion he had ever seen. The lion's mane shimmered as if dipped in gold, its eyes, giant and piercing, shined like two amber halos. Its fur was short like a normal lion except it sparkled like a bronzed statue, and its claws glistened in the sparse light like diamonds. Vegas felt a slight rumble in the ground as the great beast exhaled.

"Greetings," the great lion said, its mouth slightly open as it talked. The words came like a drawn out growl. "Much time has passed since I have seen another living creature."

"I didn't think anything in this place could talk," Vegas replied as he typed a message to maintain radio silence on his wrist communicator. If Joe needed to tell him something he would have to show it the view screen on his glasses.

The great lion laughed at Vega's comment. Vegas calculated that its laugh would've measured as a 1.5 on Earth's Richter scale.

"We, beings of Tartarus, can all speak; however, we choose not to communicate with lesser creatures—with mortals."

"Who ever said I was mortal? And why have you chosen to talk to me now, rather than attack?"

The lion laughed again; this time at about a 2.2. Vegas had to use his anti-grav shoes to float above the ground to stay upright.

"I have decided to speak to you because you are a bit of a mystery which raises many questions. How you were able to reach me, the chief among them? Are you a God?"

Vegas hesitated, but tried to play it off as being affronted. He needed a second to figure out how to play this. What do you say when a giant powerful mythological creature asks you if you're a god—

"Fuck, yeah," Vegas answered boldly. "Yes, I am a god."

"Interesting," the great lion replied. "God of what if I may ask?"

"No, you may not. Who I am is of none of your concern, lion. I only seek passage to the power that I am after."

"AAAhhh, well that changes everything then. A god seeking the power to destroy the gods, the great and limitless power, now that I am aware of your quest I have both good and bad news for you."

The arrogance in the lion's voice was seriously starting to annoy Vegas. They had barely spoken, but Vegas already wanted it dead. "Good news first," Vegas said as calmly as he could manage.

The lion stood to its full height on all four legs exposing a large set of metal doors, as well as revealing that its body was much larger than Chimera and actually made Cerberus look like a puddle.

"The path to the power you're after is just beyond this door; however, there are two challenges you must overcome. The second is beyond this door, it is what you might call an unstoppable force."

"Unstoppable force—shouldn't be a problem. What's the first challenge?" Vegas said his body language matching the bravado in his voice.

"Me, of course. I am the unmovable beast; I am the great impenetrable Nemean Lion."

"So, let me get this straight. I have to get by you in order to go through that door, and then I have to defeat some unstoppable force before I get this power?"

"You cannot get past me. You must kill me for this door to open."

"You're telling me, you want me to kill you?"

"I'm telling you that you can't kill me, so you cannot pass." The lion growled.

"My skin is impenetrable, I--"

Before the Nemean Lion could finish what he was saying, Vegas reached for the small of his back, and then pulled out a fire arrow from his quiver. In seconds, Vegas sent the arrow darting towards the lion. As the arrow reached its target, Vegas jumped back with all his might then hid behind a nearby pillar as the colossal explosion went off.

When the dust settled, Vegas peeked around the pillar and saw the lion standing as if he was just hit by a flea. The lion's mouth opened wide as it laughed hysterically, the force from the lion's breath was almost as powerful as the exploding arrow, and it seemed to shake the temples to its foundation with all of his jollity.

As the great lion laughed, Vegas read a message Joe had sent him. The message read: **Vegas, I forgot Miner told me that he knew a lot about this Greek shit. So I asked him about this Nemean Lion and he said that not a lot was known about this fucker...apparently Hercules choked the shit out of this thing. There's no other info about him and strangling it is the only way that has ever been documented to kill it. How you gonna choke that big ass thing, I don't know. Also, the only thing that could hurt him was his own claws. Hope that helps.**

God bless Robert Holley, Vegas thought as an idea crept into his head and a sinister smile etched across his lips.

Slowly Vegas pulled another arrow from his quiver then loaded it on the bow, aiming it at the great lion's head.

"You must be one of the lower gods. You are obviously an idiot. Next time a being of Tartarus tells you they're impenetrable, do not be foolish enough to attack them."

"If you open the door and let me pass now, I promise not to kill you. This is your only warning," Vegas said in a very matter of fact tone.

"You dare threaten me? You must be insane. I would've been satisfied to let you traverse the labyrinth of the temple until you died, but now for your insolence..." the lion faced Vegas and planted his feet, its claws digging into the stone ground, and its legs braced for attack. Its mouth formed a snarl and a growl that vibrated in the ground.

"You think I'm scared of you, you giant pussy cat? I'm about to beat your ass like Hercules did. I heard he punched you in the nose and you ran like a little bitch!"

"Lies!" The Nemean Lion roared, its mouth open, its teeth salivating for blood and flashing their deadly brilliance.

Without hesitation, Vegas released the arrow completely confident with the outcome. The arrow found its mark and soared into the lion's mouth where the icy explosion traveled deep into the lion's airway. Vegas didn't pretend to understand magical creatures but he knew they were consistent. If this lion had to breath on Earth it probably had to breath something here, too.

The Nemean Lion was cut off from breathing in an instant. It shook violently, and then clawed at his throat trying to crush the ice, so he could breath. However, the liquid nitrogen would have already traveled deeper in the lion; it was only a matter of time.

Vegas slowly buckled his bow back on his belt, and then walk on air toward the lion. When he was standing over the lion's body, Vegas saw it look up as its life slowly drained away.

"Next time someone tells you that they're a god and to get the fuck out of the way— get the fuck out of the way," Vegas said without a trace of pity in his voice.

Without looking back Vegas, walked toward the now opened metal doors ready to face an unstoppable force—whatever it maybe.

* * * *

Vegas had been walking for hours without running into anything resembling an unstoppable force. He had stumbled across more traps, demons, and monsters but nothing powerful enough to be considered unstoppable. For the past forty-five minutes, Vegas had been walking six feet above a lake surrounded by absolute darkness. The darkness was unlike anything Vegas had ever experienced. It was as though the dark was eating any light that presented itself. The blackness seemed to move and focus itself with purpose.

Even with his night vision glasses, Vegas could only see maybe fifty or seventy-five yards in any direction. His vision was limited; even when he modified his glove to create florescent hovering light sources with the snap of his fingers. The purple light the glove created would stay suspended in air until it dissolved within thirty seconds. It took Vegas awhile to make the light save because whatever the lake he was crossing was made of, it definitely wasn't water, because it was highly flammable.

Vegas continued to walk over the lake occasionally flicking light ahead of him or off in different directions. From what he could piece together, he was in something resembling a cave. There were stalactites piercing through the lake and Vegas could see the ends of stalagmites.

Finally Vegas thought he saw the shoreline of the lake in view, but as he approached it a wall of light erupted in front of him. Quickly, Vegas jumped back, snapped off five blooms of light in strategic positions, then slid his hands together letting the glove's energy spark and crackle, ready to summon a weapon on command.

Vegas watched as the light began to take shape forming the depth and width, form and volume, of a face. Vegas felt a weak energy coming from the light; it also felt much—older than anything else Vegas had encountered at this point. When the face had formed, Vegas still had to struggle to make out its features. Portions of the face glittered and sparkled brightly like the stars in the night sky, while other sections were blue and vibrant like a sunny afternoon.

"I am the Titan of the sky, Uranus, the first ruler of Earth and the heavens," the Titan said with a voice that reminded Vegas of rolling thunder. "You are close to the power you seek. All that remains are three battles which you must win, and then the power will be yours to do with as you please."

Vegas took stock in the situation, listened to the Titan's words, but didn't drop his guard. Vegas was careful to mask any feelings of surprise or fear from his voice, "The Nemean Lion said I only had to defeat an unstoppable force."

"Surely you didn't believe a word the lion told you. What reason did it have to tell you the truth?"

"What do you want?" Vegas demanded.

"I want you to accomplish your mission."

Now that was worth at least a raised eye brow. Vegas knew this was the temple of the Titans and he knew they had no reason to want to see their great power stolen.

"Go on," Vegas said wanting to hear what the Titan had to say, but still never dropping his guard.

"What is your name?" Uranus asked, the sun shining in one eye and moonlight gleaming in the other.

"Vegas."

"Do you know of me, Vegas? Do you know of my story?"

Vegas hesitated, waiting to see if Joe would send him any info on Uranus, but nothing flashed across his glasses. Uranus continued before Vegas had the time to come up with a lie or a bluff.

"I am the first son and the first husband of Gaia, the Titan mother of all that you know. I ruled the sky and heavens for millennia, until my youngest son, Kronus, castrated me at the command of my wife Gaia then stripped me of most of my power. Once defeated, I was then banished from Earth. I was betrayed by those closest to me, by those whom I had sworn to protect."

"That's sad. Especially the part about your son chopping your balls off," Vegas said sarcastically, "but why should I care?"

"I do not wish for your pity—only your victory. Like the gods, the Titans can no longer affect the world of men directly. However, I do have allies just as my betrayers; if you survive their next champion, I shall send you an aide to help you on your quest."

"I'm still not all that clear on why you would want to help me or if I should trust you."

"Your trust means nothing to me. God or Titan we can never die; yet we will never be able to rise to power as we once had on Earth. There is nothing I can do to strike out at those that turned against me, no way for me to hurt them worse than the pain I now endure except if you were to succeed. Even in their current state, their pride knows no end, and nothing would shatter that pride like seeing a mortal achieve something that they themselves could not."

Vegas stared at the image of the Titan, its face shifting between clear skies, fierce storms and shooting comets in the night. Vegas felt the power of his glove cycling, yearning for release just as his paranoia was churning in his gut. Within seconds Vegas was running the situation in his mind, working out every angle and possible outcome he could think of.

"I take my leave—you will never hear from me again. Prepare yourself for battle mortal, or prepare to die." Then just as suddenly as he appeared, Uranus faded away and Vegas was once again left alone in the darkness. Before Vegas could give much credence to Uranus' warning, Joe started shouting in his earpiece.

"Vegas, you need to get out of there!"

"Calm down, Joe, what's going on? What am I up against?"

Off in the distance Vegas could hear a shifting of wind. He tried to focus on it and listen to Joe at the same time.

"One of the probes just picked it up! This thing if freaking huge! Its heat signature is massive!"

"What is it?"

The cycling of air continued and grew louder and louder. Whatever it was, it was getting closer to Vegas' position.

"Holy shit! You're standing over top of a fucking A-bomb man. That whole lake is flammable isn't it? Oh, shit. Oh, shit! Vegas you gotta run—run damnit!"

"Joe, calm down! I'm not running from anything or anyone in here. Now tell me what am I up against?"

As the sound of rustling air grew louder and closer, Vegas realized what he was listening to was more of a flapping than a cycling of air. Then, two huge slits of red appeared in the distant darkness. The darkness didn't try to consume the red lights rushing towards Vegas like it did the light Vegas had created. It was as though the darkness was submitting—yielding to the red lights and the power they held.

"Oh, shit! Oh, shit!" Joe continued shrieking in Vegas' ear.

Feeling terrified, anxious and annoyed Vegas used the energy he had stored from his glove, bent it to his will then tossed it high into the air forcing the energy to act like a mini sun minus the heat. It would only stay lit for about sixty seconds, but Vegas would be able to see what he was up against.

"Damnit, Vegas, you have to run!"

"Calm the fuck down!" Vegas roared then clapped his hands together to let the energy in his glove build again.

"I've handled everything else they've thrown at me. It doesn't matter how many there are or how big I can take care of it. Why would I run now?"

"Why should you run? Why should you run!?"

The flapping grew louder and faster. The red slits Vegas now recognized as eyes grew wider with anticipation of the kill, then fire blazed from near the eyes in every shade of red, orange, blue, green and purple. Even though it was still so far away; Vegas could feel the heat from the flame. Vegas felt it was strange that he felt such admiration for the beautiful swirling colors of burning death. The flames seemed to focus themselves and collect info into a ball of orange just as the source entered Vegas' strobe light.

When Vegas got a clear look at what he was up against, it felt like his heart dropped out of his chest. His lips felt chapped, his throat was dry, his knees weak, and he knew he had only seconds to pull himself together before he was a dead man, "Oh," Vegas said expressionless.

"Yeah, oh! You gonna run now, aren't ya?" Joe screamed sarcastically, "'Cause that's a mutha fuck'n dragon bitch!"

"Bohica."

Chapter 10

"I never run!" Vegas growled as fear was stomped out by determination and doubt was bitch slapped into submission by pride. Vegas used his shoes to rocket skyward as a colossal stream of fire raced towards him faster than the wind. Even though the fire missed Vegas, he felt the flames ignite the lake below. The combustion was so intense it encompassed his surroundings as if Vegas were standing over an erupting volcano.

The lake gave off a rancid smell of burning flesh and brimstone that invaded Vegas' nostrils causing his eyes to water. The sound of the lake bursting into flames was like the grim ever reaching fingers of death struggling to place Vegas in its eternal grasp.

Above the fire raging and the mighty wings of the dragon flapping, Vegas heard a gust of wind, almost as if a giant vacuum had been turned on below him. Vegas adjusted his glasses so that the brightness from the flames wouldn't blind him, then looked down and saw the color shift in the dragon's eyes from red to blue. The vacuum sound stopped and the dragon's throat and mouth contorted until it spat out a burst of blue flames as fast as any lightning bolt.

Before the fire was launched his way, Vegas used his shoes to stop then perform a back flip that vaulted him out of the way. The blue flame zoomed by Vegas missing him by inches sounding like a dropping bomb, until it finally struck the roof of the cave far above. Vegas tried to estimate the speed and explosive force of the flame when it hit, but didn't have time before the dragon hurled another two rounds of blue flame in his direction.

Because he was walking on air instead of flying, Vegas had greater maneuverability; with several jab steps Vegas easily avoided the dragon's attacks until the dragon itself flew past Vegas. With a brief sprint, Vegas put enough distance between him and the dragon causing it to circle around in a wide angle to attack again. The dragon looked immensely powerful. Vegas had to exploit its strengths rather than its weaknesses. Staying in close and choosing the right angles would let the great beast's size work to Vegas' advantage.

Vegas used the seconds he had to activate his power glove to create another artificial light source so he could get a good look at what he was up against. He was so high above the scorching lake that its light wouldn't reach; it was like the darkness in the cavern was swallowing the light from the fire. When he tossed the light in the air, Vegas saw the dragon in all its malevolent glory. The dragon was covered in golden, deep scale-like armor, with spikes from its head to the tip of its tail. The dragon's mouth had more width than depth with large nostrils that shot out smoke as it exhaled. Its wings were thick and powerful, stretching over ten city blocks but they were oddly thin looking like a pterodactyl. From head to tail, the dragon had to be almost three miles long and its body coiled and weaved like a snake as its wings gracefully propelled it through the air.

Slamming his hands together, Vegas summoned the most destructive weapon he could produce, his Matador rocket launcher. "If you can understand me, this is your only warning! Surrender and I swear I will not kill you!" Vegas screamed at that top of his lungs. He figured it was worth a try. If a freaking lion could talk in this place, why not a dragon, right? The dragon flapped its wings fiercely pushing itself forward with a low menacing growl that echoed "You dare" was the only response Vegas' ultimatum received.

Charging closer, Vegas sent the rocket toward his enemy and watched it fly for what felt like forever before it struck between the dragon's eyes with the force of five atomic bombs. Just like the Neaman Lion, this dragon probably hadn't fought anyone since the most powerful weapons were wooden arrows and pitchforks; it was a safe bet he had never been hit with an atomic bomb before. For an instant Vegas felt a hint of pride in his resourcefulness, but quickly saw it shatter as the dragon flew through the explosion like a tank through a waterfall. Again the building sound of a vacuum started up, this time accompanied by a faint rattling, and then the dragon shot out a spray of fire more powerful than the rocket Vegas had just fired.

While standing on air, Vegas let himself fall backwards into a free fall to avoid the initial breath of fire. When he twisted in his free fall to face the dragon, Vegas saw the blazing breath was barreling down on him. Using his shoes, Vegas managed to maneuver away from the flame, but the dragon was aware of how Vegas would move now and was adjusting. One quick slide of his hands and Vegas had produced his shield, when he did the dragon seemed to recognized what it was then changed tactics.

The dragon righted itself to hover in the air; then with a sharp suck of air, a spiraling ball of flame was sent toward Vegas. His shield took the full blow, but it was enough to knock Vegas off balance and send him flying en route for the lake filled inferno below.

The blast had Vegas falling and spinning out of control, but he was able to right himself enough to catch the dragon's movement as it dove after him at full speed. Within seconds, the dragon was almost close enough to swallow Vegas whole! Vegas heard a familiar vacuum sound then felt himself being pulled into the razor sharp teeth of the dragon. He quickly placed his shield on his feet then used it to block the dragon's breath as energy crackled producing his sword, just as another blast of fire sprayed from the dragon's mouth.

Vegas twisted with the blast allowing his anti-grav shoes to carry him upward as the fire whizzed by him. Vegas grabbed the dragon's scales searching for any weak spot in its armor. He expected the dragon to shake and twist to try to throw him off, but instead it retracted its wings and dive bombed towards the lake of fire. Vegas let go just in time to stand over the flames coming from the lake. He then used his shoes to ascend avoiding his clothes catching on fire.

He had no idea what the dragon was doing, but Vegas used this time to formulate a plan. Vegas needed this to end quickly; the longer the battle went on the more he was at a disadvantage. After eight seconds of the dragon being submerged in the lake, Vegas had three plans-each more dangerous than the last and each with a high possibility Vegas wouldn't survive.

Vegas had floated high above the lake then watched the area where the dragon had dived in. The lake's fire began to shine brighter and higher as if the flame was somehow alive doing a dance of praise for Vegas' impending death. Suddenly the dragon sprung from the lake, its whole body blazing white hot as if it were dipped in lava, then it drew in air and fire from the lake using it to intensify its own power in an impressive display of pyrotechnic might.

Vegas watched the dragon rise from the lake like a monstrous demon from hell releasing a millennia of caged fury. Everything slowed for Vegas as the dragon's wings flapped; its great muscles tensed and contracted while every movement yearned for blood.

Beautiful, Vegas thought as he stared in awe of the dragon's power and a smirk etched Vegas' lips. Vegas reached for his bow, grabbed the arrow he wanted out of his quiver, and then began a swan dive into the hell that rushed to meet him.

"Time to try plan A," Vegas said to himself and wondered if this plan didn't work, would he live long enough to try the other two?

* * * *

Vegas pulled back on his bow then let his last arrow full of liquid nitrogen fly into the mountain of fire rushing towards him. As he fell, Vegas put the bow back in its place at the small of his back, then accessed the power glove to form a dagger in both hands. The arrow nullifying its fire caught the dragon off guard; Vegas was able to land on the ice and force its forward movement to slow enough for the dragon to ram into the frozen clumps. When the clumps of ice and the dragon collided, it shrieked in pain.

Using the shock to his advantage, Vegas was able to control his fall then dig deep into the dragon's hide with his daggers. Vegas held on until the dragon righted itself and then leaped for the dragon's wing, trading his daggers for his sword, in order to do maximum damage. Vegas stabbed his sword into the wing of the dragon then ran the length of the beast's wingspan, until the wing almost separated from muscle. The dragon used its long neck to twist around to spray fire at Vegas forcing him to retreat.

Vegas exchanged sword for shield then and let the force of the fire blast him a safe distance from the dragon as it flailed and clawed at anything around trying to halt its fall. Vegas stood high above the dragon and watched with a hint of triumph in his heart as the dragon found a far off cliff to break its fall. Vegas snapped his fingers with both hands producing his artificial light so that he could see the dragon wallow in agony and defeat. As he watched, Vegas found something very interesting. When it was on land, the dragon didn't move at all like Vegas would've expected. Instead of moving like a lizard or an alligator like its anatomy suggested, the dragon moved more like a lion or panther. The way it climbed on the rocks of the cave, the way its shoulders moved with its wings retracted, its tail erect waving back and forth, all screamed big fire-breathing cat climbing a tree.

However Vegas only paid minor attention to these details, because he was already trying to find his way out of the cave to find the power he needed now that he dragon was grounded. He didn't get too far in that line of thought before the dragon turned to look at Vegas and roared with so much force, the shock wave knocked him back almost causing him to lose his balance. Vegas was pushed back so far he had to use the zoom feature on his glasses to see the dragon. What he saw practically sent his heart into his throat. The dragon rose onto its hind legs then roared again with equal force, but this time with its wings extended completely healed.

The dragon's eyes fixated on Vegas then it pushed off from the cave side with so much ferocity that it created a sonic boom and left a crater in the stone. Vegas forced his heart back into his chest then stiffened his resolve. He planted his feet then slammed his hands together forcing the power in the glove to flicker, spark alive subservient to his will.

All right then, plan B.

* * * *

Plan B had a lower chance of survival than plan A, but Vegas didn't have the luxury of being picky at the moment, especially, when he was fighting a dragon that was charging him at the speed of sound. Vegas let the energy in his hands build as the dragon rushed him, but instead of bending it into a weapon, he amplified the energy until it pulsed and sparks flew off his fist.

Using the digital reading on his glasses, Vegas approximated the dragon's speed and timed the exact second he needed to juke in order to avoid the charge. With a well placed side step, Vegas was able to avoid the dragon's crushing jaws then use the energy built up in his fist to punch the dragon in its right eye. The dragon shrieked then snapped and clawed at Vegas. Instead of all out dodging the dragon, Vegas was stutter stepping its strikes then repelling them with blows of his own. Each time he made contact, the energy in his hands would pop and crack loudly creating sparks like a lighting hammer striking a thunder anvil.

The dragon seemed to grow more and more ferocious with every blow Vegas landed. Each time it went for Vegas, the dragon's body language oozed frustration with its every miss. Vegas began implanting his plan by landing a blow on the dragon then retreating, then coming in close, and then retreating again. Vegas was able to stand in place in the air, but the dragon had to frantically flap its wings and expend more energy to hover in place. When Vegas had the dragon fighting under his terms, he began to shoot with his shotgun as he retreated trying to entice another blast of fire. The whole time he attacked, Vegas ran calculations and measurements in his head; if his plan was going to work, he needed perfect timing and perfect execution.

Finally as Vegas retreated and heard the vacuum preparing for another fire blast, instantly he snapped his fingers tossing one of his artificial suns into the dragon's mouth. Vegas worked the formula in his mind to produce a large spark of light that wouldn't just give off light, but would also burn and act as a high-powered accelerant to any surrounding flame. When the dragon swallowed the light, its fire breath ignited causing a white-hot burst of energy and flames. Vegas quickly used the power glove to punch the dragon in the snout then zoomed upward.

When he felt he was at a safe distance, Vegas stopped then used his glasses to zoom in on the dragon. The plan was to use the dragon's fire against him, with the artificial sun and the accelerant formula to speed up, intensify and prolong the dragon's natural power, burning it up from the inside—at least that was the theory. Instead, the dragon coughed and spat out fire into all directions. It was almost as though the dragon was secreting fire like a normal person sweating profusely. Instead of being damaged, the dragon looked like a living white-hot ball of flame again.

The dragon again caught sight of Vegas then rushed him with more intensity than ever. Vegas sighed deeply collapsing over, his hands on his knees. Vegas calmly took off his glasses then lightly touched two fingers to his left temple as the dragon drew nearer.

Ok, all or nothing. Plan C.

* * * *

Once he felt power cycling through his eyes, Vegas ran behind a near by stalactite and prepared himself for his final gambit. This was his last chance to defeat the dragon; if this didn't work, he was dead and so was the universe. Even though it was far away, Vegas could feel the dragon speeding towards him. He could hear it cut through the air, sounding like a speeding freight train. Vegas could see the light from the dragon completely engulfed in flames and getting closer like a living comet.

Just like he planned, the dragon bursted through the stalactite, wings spread and fangs flashing, Vegas retreated and then used his shoes to propel himself downward. The dragon advanced falling for Vegas' ruse of retreat until Vegas turned and released the awesome power that had built in his eyes.

Years ago, Vegas discovered a dimension made up of nothing but kinetic energy. Vegas had nearly destroyed Earth when he stumbled across the dimension that day, but he was able to harness its energy. Releasing the power of an exploding star directly in the face of the dragon, he created an explosion that rocked the entire temple. Even though Vegas had discovered how to rob the blast of its inertia, making it a repulsion blast with a reactionless one way push allowing him to deliver the blast without being forced hundreds of miles backwards, it was still a struggle to hold his ground using it on this scale.

The dragon didn't have a chance to react or even scream in pain as it was hit by the concussion blast and shattered into pieces like a deer hit by an eighteen-wheeler going ninety on the freeway. Vegas had to focus his will with everything he had to shut down the stream of energy before it leaked out into our dimension and destroyed everything. He felt the avatar grow weak, his vision became blurry, as he fell toward the lake of fire below. Vegas turned as he fell and was helpless to stop his impending plunge into the lake of fire, then as he got closer Vegas watched as all the fire in the lake collected into one massive shape then rushed upward to meet him. The fire formed a—bird, as far as what Vegas could tell, and it shrieked like a great and powerful eagle.

The bird made of flames opened its mouth swallowing Vegas whole. The last thing Vegas remembered was a warm comforting feeling of falling into nothingness, of finally being able to rest as he descended into the blazing light.

* * * *

Vegas should have been dead, the avatar burnt to a crisp, but instead he woke up floating on his back in the lake. Vegas pulled himself up and let his shoes lift him a foot above the lake listening to his surroundings. He had no idea what had happened or how he was still alive, let alone, how the avatar was still functional. Using that optic star blast was dangerous on Earth, but it should have drained the avatar of all its energy unless he worked the equations just right—even if the equations were right; it should have taken him hours to be able to move. Vegas checked his timer display on his wrist and found only minutes had passed, not hours! Not only had the avatar been restored but the flammable lake was renewed as if a spark had never touched it. It didn't make any sense.

Vegas reset his glove to produce the non-flammable light sources then snapped several to life around him. Off in the distance, there were different chunks of the dragon that had been obliterated into pieces by the star burst. A smirk edged Vegas' lips as he saw the body parts of the dragon sprawled out over the lake; he also noticed a dim light far off in the distance where his star blast had punched through the temple, beginning its endless journey into the cosmos.

"Vegas! Vegas are you all right? What the hell happened?" Vegas heard Joe shout in his ear as soon as he unmuted his end.

"I kicked a dragon's ass that's what happened," Vegas replied, grinning and popping his knuckles.

"Bullshit! Just cause you couldn't hear me screaming like a bitch, which I probably was, doesn't mean I didn't see the fight. You got fucking lucky! I mean what happened, as in you were dying over here, and then you suddenly sprung back to life. Plus, you were overheating like a mother fucker. I was pouring buckets of ice water on you, but I still thought your brain was going to melt."

Vegas paused thinking over what Joe was saying. "How high was my body temperature?"

"Computer said it was up to like one twelve! I thought a person became a vegetable if they got that hot."

"Normally yes, but I built safe guards in the avatar to prolong my brain functions in circumstances like that. However, if they did the job, I shouldn't be feeling so good so soon. I feel better than I did when I first landed on the planet; something else kept me alive."

Suddenly, before Vegas and Joe's conversation could continue, a faint light accompanied by a dull force of weak energy floated in front of Vegas in the shape of a giant head much in the same fashion Uranus had appeared earlier. Only this head was a lot uglier than Uranus. Its forehead was huge and slumped back, its small eyes seemed set back farther in the skull than a normal person's. Its nose was much too small for its head, centered just below the middle of its two narrow eyes. It had a long jaw and mouth and had deep wrinkles etched around the eyes, cheeks and mouth. Some how the ears were large, but they still looked small and out of proportion.

"I am the Titan Kronus!" the head said, in a voice that Vegas found more comical than threatening, like Michael Clark Duncan trying to do a gay British accent.

Vegas fought to keep himself from laughing before replying, "So?"

Vegas had some knowledge of Kronus. He was the Titan of time and ruled the world after killing his father Uranus. He had several brothers who had ruled with him and he had several children with his wife, who was also his mother, Gaea.

"You are an arrogant, insolent whelp who does not know his place! You shall not leave this temple alive! So swears Kronus, Titan of time!"

"Your daddy already gave me the rundown on you Titans. I know you can't touch me from wherever you are, so don't write a check that your ass can't cash buddy," Vegas said as if the Titan's threats were no more dangerous than a fly on the wall.

"You dare underestimate me? You dare presume yourself more powerful than the immortal power of the Titan's mortal? We cannot be killed, only vanquished to the depths of Tarsaus from which we will always rise. The small faction of power we now possess in our eternal slumber is enough to kill you where you stand."

"So you say," Vegas replied, "yet here I still stand."

Vegas felt the Titan's essence become stronger in front of him as his anger grew, "Just because my pitiful father dispatched a phoenix to restore you doesn't not mean—"

"Look, fuck you. Fuck your small ass nose and gargoyle looking face. Fuck your Titan of time bullshit. Fuck your gay ass accent. Fuck you for cutting your dad's nuts off. Fuck your crusty face. But most importantly just fuck you, you literal mother fucker having kids with your own mother, you sick fuck! You ain't shit, and you can't do shit!"

Vegas said then walked past the projection of Kronus in the direction of the power he was after, "Now, excuse my back." Vegas was a few steps away from land when the Titan finally spoke.

"You fool!"

"I'm sorry," Vegas said sticking up his middle finger as he walked, "but I can't hear you over the sound of how epic I am."

"Do you think we have no knowledge of the modern world? We are aware of how you stand before us in our temple. Though you may fight though our protectors; we know you are not without aids of your own. You will die this day—I never mentioned how."

When Vegas turned the projection of Kronus had disappeared but his cold, malicious laugh echoed throughout the cavern like a nefarious bell ringing for the walking dead.

Vegas' heart dropped as he caught the meaning of Kronus' threat. They knew what he was and how he was here. *They're going after the guys!* Vegas thought, as he turned then sprinted in the direction of life's ambition—limitless power. Vegas touched his earpiece to warn Joe and the others, hoping he wouldn't be too late.

Chapter 11

Robert Holley was tired, hot, and sweating like a hooker in church as he stood in front of the massive god particle machine. He had no idea how it worked and couldn't care less; all he knew was he had to keep magma gushing up through the bottom of this thing until Vegas could finish doing whatever the hell he was doing. Rob had long since lost track of time and of his patience. He had helped Vegas save Earth several times since getting his power and helping Vegas save the universe left him feeling the same. It was a lot like pissing yourself with dark pants on—it's a warm feeling, but nobody notices.

Not only was Rob using all his energy to keep this contraption running; but he kept being asked questions about Greek mythology and everyone seemed shocked that he actually knew the answers. If that was the case, why ask someone a question if you didn't think they would know the answer? It was just insulting! He just didn't understand physics and all this other space crap, but that didn't mean he was stupid. He had a teaching degree in science for crying out loud!

Still Rob couldn't complain too much. He was after all standing where no other man had ever stood and seeing what no other man had ever seen. Rob had grown up in Southern West Virginia before he moved to Las Vegas and he had always read about and seen pictures of the Alaskan Auras. The damn things had always fascinated him so much that he had put seeing them on top of his bucket list, but now he could cross them off. As Io's highly charged atmosphere passed through Jupiter's shadow and its massive magnetosphere, it gave birth to the most spectacular Auras Rob could have imagined.

It was like the entire sky was alive with a blanket waving colors more vibrant than any rainbow on Earth. It was a welcome change. Rob thought he was going to burst a blood vessel in his forehead from getting so mad having to look up and see Jupiter. He had gained control of the pull the two moons, Ganymede and Europa, had on Io but Jupiter's hold was massive and relentless.

"Miner! Miner, you there?" Rob heard Joe scream in his earpiece.

"Of course, I'm here! Where ya expect me ta go, kid? What's up?"

"Vegas said the gig is up. He's been beating down everything the Titan's have thrown at him and now they don't want to play fair any more. Vegas thinks they're going to start coming after us since they can't kill him."

"He sure? Everything look'n da same so far."

"No, he's not sure actually. Vegas just said that was the impression Kronus gave him."

"Kronus?" Rob barked, "Vegas ran into Kronus, the Titan of time?"

"That's who he said he was, yeah, how'd you know that?"

Rob paused. "Son, I'm start'n ta think you ain't got the good sense God gave a pigeon."

"What?"

"Just tell me what to expect." Rob sighed swallowing his anger.

"Again not sure. VB just wanted me to warn you and big O. I'm having a hard time getting through to big O so I'm letting you know first. I am picking up a lot of movement from something the ship computer calls the Kuiper Belt at the edge of the solar system. It says something is coming this way, but I'm not sure what it means. Any ideas?"

"Nope. Only thing I'm think'n about is keep'n this here motor runn'n."

"I really wish I had more time to learn about this ship. Vegas was so obsessed with me learning to fly this thing I didn't learn what most of these buttons and switches do. You have no idea what I've been going through in here by myself it's like—"

"Wo, wo, wo, son I ain't got a dog in that fight. You're gonna have to figure that out on your own."

"By the way, Vegas wanted to make sure you guys knew that the Titans can't attack directly. He didn't say why they couldn't or how he knew, but he seemed positive. He wanted you to make sure not to let their theatrics intimidate you."

Suddenly the ground of Io began to rumble, moving violently up and down like a blanket in the wind. Rob was in tunc with most of the moon and he could feel it bursting in several directions.

"What's going on?" Joe asked. "I'm picking up an energy spike on Io—I think."

"Get on the horn with Deep and tell him to get ready to be attacked. He'll need the warning! Tell Vegas I'll keep this thing juiced up as long as I can!" Rob shouted then turned off his earpiece. Rob knew he was alone now. There was no one who could help him; no one could back him up or come to his rescue if he failed. Rob knew what was at stake. He knew if he didn't keep the machine running as long as he could the universe was dead.

Even though Rob knew that, he didn't care. He didn't know the whole damn universe, so he couldn't fight for something he didn't know and couldn't grasp. Instead for the first time since Vegas called him to his apartment, Rob let himself think of his wife Charish. He thought about how she begged him not to go because she didn't trust Vegas, because she knew how dangerous the missions Vegas gave him often were. Rob remembered not wanting to go. He remembered how he wanted to stay in bed with his wife wrapped in his arms.

Then, as the moon Io began to shake more violently around him and its surface began to glow with ghostly reds, oranges, and yellows just as brilliant as the Aurous above, Rob remembered why he went when Vegas called. Rob remembered why he helped Vegas save the planet all those times. Even though the whole fucking world may not ever notice the risk he took, his wife always did. Screw the world and fuck the goddamn universe. Rob was fighting for his wife! If Titans were threatening this machine, they were threatening Charish! It didn't matter if it was a Titan, God, angel or demon, whatever hell they threw at him Rob swore it wouldn't be anything compared to the hell he was about to raise.

Slamming his ax into the ground strengthening his hold on the moon Rob shouted, "Let's see what ya mutha fuckers got!"

* * * *

Rob didn't have control over the whole moon, but he could feel its entire surface and what he felt let him know that what he was seeing was as real as it was terrifying. Rob stood with his back to the god particle machine as hundreds of thousands of molten forms rose from the moon's surface. Each individual mound of the moon grew until it was seven feet tall, forming arms, legs, a torso, and head out of solid rock.

Rob dug his shoes into the ground to get a better sense of his surroundings. From what he could tell, the rock creatures were forming on the half of the moon closest to Jupiter ignoring the sections of the moon where Rob's influence was strongest. Rob was thankful he had spent so much time pulling Io from Ganymede and Europa. If he hadn't, the rock creatures would have him completely surrounded and it would only be a matter of time before he was overwhelmed. At least this way, Rob had a fighting chance.

The first wave of molten men raised their arms and each hurled a fire ball at Rob. Using his control over the ground, Rob stomped his foot forcing the ground around him upward blocking the barrage of flaming rocks. Then he countered by swinging his axe pushing the rock into his enemies with unbelievable speed and force. Instead of waiting for the rock monsters to advance on him, Rob charged the multitude, axe held high screaming a war cry at the top of his lungs.

Rob had trained with Vegas and sparred extensively with Deep, but no matter how much training he received, he always fought the same way. Once a reporter asked Rob to describe his fighting style and he had answered, "I curse a lot'n swing a big stick!" Which was exactly what Rob was doing now that he had charged headlong into the army that threatened his mission.

Though he must have looked like a wild animal lashing out, Rob did have a plan. He wanted to put more room between the molten army and the god particle machine, which also gave him more room to retreat and regroup if he needed to. He swung his axe wildly using every expletive he could think of, he even made up a few, sending rocks and boulders flying in all directions as he swung his weapon. He opened canyon to crush his enemies and flung chucks of the moon as big as mountain ranges with a powerful wave of his axe.

Within seconds, Rob had cleared a good mile of territory for himself without even breaking a sweat! He kept the pressure on forcing the rock army back farther and farther, until he saw something that almost made him wish he were a kid again back home gulping down a dose of Similac.

The rock army started to come together like one large molten flow of lava. Rob had to fight off smaller pieces that where still attacking, but a bulk of the army was concentrating their efforts into coming together. Rob could feel what they were doing. Even as he fought, he could feel his new foe take shape until it stood almost two hundred feet tall!

Great, now I gotta fight fuck'n Voltron!

Rob quickly opened a mile-wide crevice into the surface of Io then retreated closer to the god particle machine where his powers were strongest. Rob knew the hole in the ground wouldn't buy him much time, but he needed a second to catch his breath. The rock monster that had formed seemed unbelievably tall. The creature had no face, just a head with two arms, a large round boulder in place of his fist, and legs and feet that threatened to flatten Rob like an ant. As if that wasn't enough, more of the smaller molten men that he saw before started to appear.

Seeing how badly the odds were stacked against him, Rob simply sighed deeply. He would've been surprised, but with his luck, this is exactly what he expected. It wouldn't be a mission to save the world if Robert Holley wasn't getting screwed in the ass somehow.

"Bohica," Rob whispered. If that phrase didn't apply to any other person on Earth it definitely applied to Rob.

Rob felt sorry for himself for a solid five seconds before he stiffened his resolve. So the universe was screwing him again, he could either cry about it or save his wife—Rob chose his wife.

A stampede of enemies charged his position, yet Rob stood his ground, "Aw'ight then!" He grunted. After that. he attacked the living mountain and the molten men army a second time. This time however—he had no intentions of retreating.

Chapter 12

Deep Willis was mentally exhausted. Drilling through the ice was repetitious and became harder the deeper Deep got to the 'potential' oceans below the ice. Deep's thoughts kept cycling over and over to why Vegas would have him doing this when there was no guarantee an ocean of water would lie under the ice of Europa. As hard as he tried, Deep couldn't figure out Vegas' reasoning. The thing was that this wasn't the first time he had done something Vegas suggested without fully understanding it, which had always worked out before. Deep had come to trust Vegas, if not for his morals than for his intelligence.

Deep tried to keep himself grounded and focused on the task, but it was difficult. Looking up into the sky on Earth was a completely different experience than looking at the sky on Europa. Deep was still positioned where sunlight was hitting the moon, but without an atmosphere, standing on a moon left him with an almost overwhelming sense of loneliness. Everything seemed so empty as if nothing existed but the sun, Jupiter, the icy moon under his feet, and the drill—there was definitely the damn drill. There were no stars visible in the sky because of the sun's influence; the sky was a colossal void of nothingness, an empty dark vacuum tugging on Deep's mind and soul. The abyss of space sucked away everything, creating the maddening noise of nonexistence to the point that Deep was almost afraid to talk from fear that the great void would claim his voice. His situation was made more bearable when he could see the lights from the energy the god particles created giving Vegas access to the planet's surface, but now even that was gone as Europa continued its natural orbit.

The longer it took and the deeper he drilled, Deep felt more and more disconnected from reality. He felt alone and away from everything he cared about, from everything he was fighting for. It was getting to the point where Deep was starting to question his own thoughts. He felt himself going insane. Struggling to maintain his composure, Deep forced himself to fixate on what he could control, and the only thing he could control was his actions.

Push one switch around the drill, lift and slam the other. Push, lift, slam. Push, lift, slam. Push, lift, slam. Finally Deep slammed the gears as hard as he could and the drill lit up like a Christmas tree. Deep read the panels and saw the drill said that he had actually hit water! Other components of the machine started to move and power up that Deep hadn't even noticed before, then he saw an indicator letting him know that the two fuel cells were charging up. A digital display said it would only take twenty minutes for them both to be completely charged.

Deep tried to use his intercom to signal Joe to get ready to fly the ship in to load the fuel cells, but when he turned it on there was nothing but static on the other end. Deep was immediately concerned because communications with the others had been seamless until now. Joe had just updated him on Vegas' progress, or had that happened hours ago? Deep couldn't be sure, his sense of time was off, his sense of everything off. A type of fear and lonely desperation crept into Deep's mind just as water would fill a balloon and feelings of safety and purpose drained away like sand in an hourglass.

The bright icy surface under his feet, a shining ball of fire billions of miles away that he couldn't look near from fear of going blind, and a giant planet of swirling gas was all there was to Deep. No sounds, no motions, no change, only the huge drill that had come to represent labor on a scale Deep had never thought possible. Deep sat a small distance away from the drill and watched its different lights and gadgets work. He knew the machine was important, but he hated the damn thing and couldn't wait until he never had to see it again. He wanted to take his eyes off it but he couldn't, there was literally nothing else to look at, nothing else for him to do. Deep sighed heavily wishing something would happen. Suddenly, without warning—Deep got his wish.

* * * *

The ice under Deep began to rumble and shake like continents drifting apart. Ice mountains started to crumble giving way to great rifts in Europa's surface. With all the carnage unfolding around him Deep's eyes were drawn upward where the entire massive planet of Jupiter was glowing a slight red and dozens of tiny lights flashed to life in the planet's shadow representing the intensified explosions on Io.

"Rob," Deep muttered more concerned for his friend than himself.

The luxury of being concerned for someone else was quickly taken away as massive clumps of ice, some almost a mile wide slowly rained down around Deep from where they were forced into the sky. Gravity on Europa was very weak, but it was enough to pull the icy boulders back down as well as let Deep run and jump without floating away in his Obsidian form. Not that Deep had anywhere to run, but he knew he needed to protect the fuel cells or all the work he had done would be in vain. He needed a plan and needed it fast.

Deep found a block of ice falling from the sky smaller than the rest, maybe seventy to a hundred feet wide, and sprinted to put himself in position where it would land. The ice hit Deep much faster and harder than he thought it would—driving him down into the moon's frozen surface. Taking the impact strengthened his Obsidian form making it much harder, which made Deep much stronger. Using his legs and the momentum of the ice's fall, Deep pushed up with enough strength to send the tonnage of ice drifting into space.

Jumping out of the crater created by the ice block, Deep raced toward whatever was launching the ice in all directions. He had no idea what he would find, but he knew he had to try something to stop this or the fuel cells would be destroyed. Before he got close to where the ice was launched into the air, Deep stopped dead in his tracks. With amazing strength and ferocity, a monster with nine heads burst through the surface of Europa. Its heads roared, screamed and shrieked with fury and bloodlust, which really freaked Deep out since he was standing on a dead ice rock with no atmosphere in space. Hearing the monster's roars just reminded him he was dealing with something very powerful and very unnatural. Some of the heads fixated on Deep right away, while the others seemed to explore its surroundings.

Finally the monster decided that Deep was the most interesting thing around, so it charged him at full speed. The monster looked like some freakish mix of a dog and a dragon: it had four limbs and a long tail. Its body was made of thick plates of scales like armor; each head looked like a dragon with a long snout, evil eyes, and teeth salivating for blood. As quickly as he could, Deep darted to the right just as the monster's first head snapped at him.

Deep rolled with his momentum then snatched the next head that attacked him, clutching it with all his might in both arms. Deep then ran to his right hoping to take some of the heads out of the fight. The plan might have worked if he was fighting the monster on Earth, but on the low gravity of Europa, it was easy for the Hydra to twist and shake Deep off sending him hurtling through space. When Deep realized his mistake, it was already too late. He was drifting off into the great void, the absolute nothingness of space. At that instant Deep was more terrified than he had ever been in his life, the thought of floating aimlessly in space with no hope of being found or rescued was enough to make him consider deactivating his Obsidian form and letting the cold airless abyss claim his life.

Thankfully he turned and when he did, he saw large clumps of ice still hovering above the moon's surface. His fear disappeared as he thought about what Vegas would do in a situation like this. He thought how Vegas would've made fun of him for thinking about giving up, even for a second. Deep was one of the strongest beings on Earth and, while not on Vegas' level, very smart in his own right. He would figure out a way to survive—to win.

Grinning, Deep grabbed one of the larger ice clusters then swung it towards the planet while he still held on. Using his strength and calculating the geometry like he would in a game of pool, Deep twisted three hundred sixty degrees forcing the ice block towards the monster. The block of ice was large enough that it hit all nine heads causing it to stumble back dazed and wounded. Then as the momentum of his throw was sending him farther from Europa, it also sent him closer to another ice block. This time Deep used his feet to push the ice into space sending himself back to the surface. Then he twisted in the air until he faced the dark void of space and clapped his hands together with all his might.

The force he generated was nothing compared to what would happen on Earth, but it still sent Deep crashing onto the moon's icy landscape. He grabbed hold and dug his hands into the ice then looked up into space and chortled, pleased with himself for crushing his fear as easily as he could crush the ice at his finger tips. Having powers was still new to him. Even after all this time, he was always amazed at how much having confidence in himself would let him accomplish.

Deep pressed his advantage and charged at the monster, but hesitated when he noticed that the blow he landed with the ice rock had severed one of the monster's heads. Then Deep watched as two heads were birthed in its place.

This is the Hydra! Deep realized and his mind went into overdrive. How the hell could he beat something that could re-grow its heads? Plus, Deep was sure this thing was supposed to be poisonous. But Deep wasn't worried, because he couldn't be poisoned in his Obsidian form—at least he thought he couldn't. If there was ever a time Deep wished he could talk to Rob, this was it. Rob would definitely know how to kill this thing.

However, maybe Deep didn't need to kill the Hydra at all. Just seconds before Deep was almost lost forever into the far regions of space, he wondered why couldn't he use something like that to his advantage? Plus back in ancient times, people didn't have any other option but to try and cut this thing's heads off. Maybe he could just bash its heads in or something. With new found confidence, Deep ran at the Hydra feeling like a juggernaut until the Hydra revealed its trump card.

Deep heard a hiss and a rattle come from the Hydra, and then several of its heads sprayed out fire so hot it burned through another layer of his Obsidian form. As if this thing growling in space wasn't enough, it also had to find some way to breathe fire which was backed by a much stronger force then Deep expected. It took everything he could do to stay anchored on the moon and not be blown away. Out of the corner of his eye, Deep was able to see that the Hydra was also shooting fire at the ice under the fuel cells. The intense blaze, under the already weak ice, caused the whole drill to fall deep inside Europa's dark frigid waters.

The angle of the fire changed, but before Deep could react to adjust himself the Hydra was on top him. Its massive foot stomped him repeatedly while its fire burned through the ice rock. The poundings didn't hurt Deep, but they did keep him in place and stopped him from fighting back. After only a few seconds, Deep felt himself falling farther and farther into the moon. There was no other sound as he was stomped through the ice and blasted with fire—only the sounds of the Hydra snarling and roaring on top of him as each head took turns trying to rip him apart.

As the two combatants plunged into the pitch black heated waters in the depths of Europa, Deep could see the lights from the drill and the fuel cells in the distance. The Hydra continued its onslaught gnawing and tearing away at Deep's Obsidian body and still blasting fire at him all at once. Deep fought back as hard as he could, but he had lost all momentum in the battle. As the fuel cells fell into darkness off in the distance, so did Deep's hope of ever seeing anyone and anything he loved again.

Chapter 13

The power of the phoenix Uranus sent not only saved Vegas' life, it also saved the mission. The avatar's core and weapons cash were fully recharged except for the arrows. He even found a way to customize his weapons a little more thanks to the added power. It was as if the phoenix had hit a reset button for his entire tech arsenal! While it annoyed Vegas that he truly needed the help in the first place, he was still thankful. He was too close to his goal to let pride get in his way.

Vegas had traveled deeper and deeper into the temple; by his measurements he had almost traveled the distance from one coast to another in North America. Along the way he fought dozens of monsters, each more powerful than the last. By the time he reached the central chamber, Vegas' weapon reserves were almost depleted again. All his heavy ordnance was used up for a second time leaving him only with his hand-to-hand weapons: his shotgun and 45s. From this point on Vegas may have to relay heavily on phoenix's power to customize the nannites. Finally, Vegas reached the gateway for the central chamber to the entire temple. He entered very cautiously since the room was empty. His experience in the temple told him there had to be traps or something powerful laying in wait for him.

This room was much different than any other he had been in so far. Vegas walked on air twenty feet from the ground to help avoid any traps as he entered a long hallway that had different mosaics on either side of the walls. On the far end of the hallway was a set of massive doors made of some shimmering blue metal. Built into the walls on each side of the hallway were different sets of machines and turning gears. All around him mechanical devices were stoking fires, but the fire wasn't producing heat, it was more like some kind of primal energy that was being piped throughout the temple. The long hallway smelled like rust and oil from an ancient world. The air was thick with on ozone of antediluvian properties Vegas had never experienced—like walking into a room that had been undisturbed since the dawn of time.

On the opposite side of hallway was a massive machine unlike anything Vegas had ever seen or even dreamed of. Vegas took a reading from the machine with his power glove and saw that whatever this device was and whatever it did, it gave off enough energy to birth a star into life. However, the thing Vegas thought was most amazing was the fact that the machine also didn't give away any heat; instead, it kept all that power contained and controlled.

The machine had ancient looking gears and switches along with a crude mix of modern technology and technology that looked hundreds of years of ahead of anything on Earth. The machine was beautifully crafted; it was almost impossible for Vegas to tell where science ended and magic began. Yet, Vegas was in awe of the fact that even though the power and tech in front of him was unlike anything he had ever dreamed, his probes were indicating the power beyond the blue metallic doors made this look as powerful as the light off the ass end of a firefly. The bad part was that the power beyond the door was something Vegas could only describe as potential energy. It was definitely there, but it needed to be released or set free.

Vegas felt energized as he approached the blue doors. Finally he was in the home stretch; finally his life ambition was within his grasp. If he used the phoenix's power to boost the nannites, he was sure he could come up with something that would work. All he had to do was get past a set of doors—compared to everything else he'd faced today, how hard could that be?

Vegas was sprinting towards the doors when his question was answered. Somehow Vegas hadn't noticed the figure that had propped itself against the doors—a sentry standing in wait for any challenger to test its power. As Vegas drew closer, the sentinel's shape and form came into his view and he realized what he was up against; the last adversary to challenge Vegas was none other than the Minotaur.

Vegas almost chuckled. He didn't understand why a Minotaur would be appointed by the Titans to guard the entrance to limitless power. It was like the Minotaur and dragon had swapped places for the day. Vegas couldn't help but feel a little insulted that the dragon wasn't here instead of the Minotaur—until he took a closer look at his foe.

The eyes of the Minotaur had the same primal brutality as all the other monsters in the temple, but there was something intelligent in its eyes that let Vegas know he wasn't dealing with brute strength alone.

The Minotaur took several paces towards Vegas before stopping as if saying, "You will not cross this point." Then it brandished its two double-sided battle-axes. The beast had on black armor that covered its torso and back, as well as a helmet that sat on top of its head highlighting its sharp massive horns. Its battle armor was enhanced by shoulder protection, as well as protection for its legs and arms. At first glance, there seemed to be no weakness at all in the Minotaur's defenses. Its stance was confident and strong, its grip on its weapons was absolute, and its wrist dangled agile and controlled. Vegas noticed the Minotaur's eyes were devoid of emotion, cold and calculating. The scariest thing was that Vegas felt like he was looking into a mirror as a chill crept up his spine.

For a beast with the head and legs of a bull, the Minotaur had very human characteristics. Suddenly Vegas realized the danger the Minotaur represented. This was the first foe he faced in the temple that would fight like a man rather than a savage beast. It would be much more cunning and unpredictable than the others.

Vegas ran through calculations and scenarios in his head. He took a quick inventory in his mind of his remaining weapons trying to decide which would be the best to start with. Vegas was caught between an offensive choice and a defensive one, until the Minotaur lost his patience and forced Vegas's hand. Both axes in hand the Minotaur stretched out his arms as wide as he could, then roared at the sky like an enraged bull before sprinting towards Vegas with so much force its hooves left broken pieces of the ground in his wake. Its exploding fury mixed with murderous intent which was laced with efficiency and poise.

Vegas kneeled to the ground as he brushed his hands together feeling the energy cycle in his left hand as he shaped and molded it to his will producing his weapon of choice.

Defense first, Vegas thought as his shield formed in his hands just in time to absorb the Minotaur's first blow.

* * * *

Even when Vegas took the strike from the Minotaur's axe at an angle and twisted, deflecting its full force, it still chipped and slightly dented his shield. Whatever these axes were composed of, they almost made his titanium shield look like it was made of tin! Vegas dodged, peered, and twisted in a death dance avoiding the Minotaur's blows, its axes occasionally making contact with Vegas' shield sending gold and silver sparks in all directions. The vibrations from the blows sent chills through Vegas' bones. Vegas started on defense in order to gauge the monster's strength and skill, but that quickly proved to be a very bad idea. The monster pressed its advantage almost as if it had sensed Vegas' plan and was insulted at the implication that he was something to be toiled with.

Vegas tried to retreat and take to the air using his shoes, but every time he made the attempt, the Minotaur would find a way to stop him. Vegas even tried to switch weapons twice since the fight started, but the Minotaur would find a way to prevent Vegas from brushing his hands together and bending its energies to his will.

Except for its war-cry when the fight began, the Minotaur had been deafly silent. It didn't bark, grunt, snort, howl, or roar; it just kept coming! Within the first ninety seconds of this fight, Vegas had more wounds, scars and tattered pieces of clothing than he had sustained the whole time he was in the temple. In a move of desperation, Vegas faked a slip in his footing and the Minotaur went for the killing blow, raising its axe high then slamming it down with unbelievable speed and force that created a crater in the floor while birthing a loud boom and silver crackles of energy. If Vegas hadn't planned his move ahead of time, he wasn't sure he could have avoided the blow. Instead, he back flipped using the force of the near miss as an opportunity to let his hands touch so he could exchange defense for offense.

Vegas landed hard on the ground, his broad sword shimmering in the light of the massive power machines to his back. Vegas elected not to overuse his gravity shoes. If getting this power was going to mean anything to him later, he had to feel like he had earned it. Vegas looked at the Minotaur to observe its reaction to his change in weapon and got a nasty surprise. The Minotaur's eyes began to glow a pale blue, its muscles seemed to tighten, and its breathing became more intense. Somehow the Minotaur was feeding off the thick ozone all around them. Vegas could feel power flowing into the Minotaur like air forced into a vacuum. The Minotaur roared like an insane bull, and then slapped its axes together sparking to life a ethereal crackling blue energy that surrounded the axes—then the monster charged again.

Vegas felt it was finally time to tap into the phoenix forced still lodged in the nannites. As the Minotaur charged Vegas tossed his sword into the air, clapped his hands together, caught the sword in his right hand, then touched the humming energy in his left hand to the sword's guard and ran it along the blade transferring the energy. Vegas planted his feet then ran his hand across his eyes producing his dark glasses just before the Minotaur reached him.

The Minotaur lashed out at Vegas with one arm. When axe and sword collided, blue and crimson energies mixed into purple then were forced into opposite directions. The clash of power lit up the combatants' surroundings and the smell of ozone burning penetrated the air. Combining energy created booms of thunder that echoed through the corridor. With its free hand, the Minotaur went for another killing strike threatening to cut Vegas in half. Vegas twisted his wrist and then jumped using the Minotaur's mighty arm as leverage to flip and avoid the strike. Instantly the beast swung the arm Vegas was holding. Vegas twisted, but the axe still slashed him just below his temple. He used his twist to deliver his own killing blow on the Minotaur's head attempting to slice it down the middle. Right away, Vegas could feel the only thing he had killed was the Minotaur's helmet. The near miss left Vegas open so the Minotaur used its other arm to swing at Vegas like a tennis player hitting an overhand serve. Vegas used his shoes and gained just enough control to block the blow with his sword, but the force from the purple sparks sent Vegas flying backwards.

Vegas landed and rolled too many times to count, thankful he didn't cut off his head with his own sword before he jammed the sword into the ground to slow himself. When Vegas looked up, the Minotaur was gone. Feeling something descending on top of him, Vegas quickly dove to the right narrowly avoiding the Minotaur and slamming down on his back. With the sound of thunder and shaking of an earthquake, sparks of energy and shattered pieces of the ground flew in all directions. The force was so strong in momentarily lifted Vegas off the ground and sent him rolling again. Sensing another charge, Vegas brushed his hands together, switched his sword to the right hand, and then summoned his shield in his left just in time for the next assault. Vegas planted his feet then turned the sword in a downward position using it for defense instead of the shield; red and purple lightning danced around Vegas as his muscles strained and his bones fought to absorb the impact. Vegas struggled with all his strength not to collapse under the beast's outrageous vigor.

Seeing an opening, Vegas attacked the monster's hoof with his shield breaking his foe's balance. The Minotaur stumbled back and Vegas pressed his advantage with a kick to its knee. Then, Vegas again made contact, sword to axe, to use the weight of the Minotaur's own weapons to knock him further off balance. In an attempt to regain ground, the Minotaur swung with everything it had to create some distance with an unblockable blow. Vegas stutter-stepped back, but quickly threw his shield like a Frisbee clipping the Minotaur's knee again, keeping his advantage.

Again the Minotaur slipped and again Vegas went for a killing blow to the head, yet once again he failed. The Minotaur was saved by its own speed and agility as Vegas' sword sliced off one of its horns instead. Vegas had considered he would miss, so as he swung the sword his hands touched allowing Vegas to form his shotgun in his hand opposite the sword. Not giving the Minotaur time to register the change, Vegas quickly fired the shotgun into the monster's chest. Using the momentum he built up, Vegas charged swinging his sword, cutting one of the Minotaur's axes at the shaft rendering it useless.

Enraged, the Minotaur swung its remaining axe, which Vegas barely ducked under, but as he did his hands made contact and his shotgun morphed into his 45. Vegas popped off a single shot that connected with the Minotaur's left eye. The sudden pain caused the beast to slash out blindly. Vegas used his shoes to jump over the next blow twisting in the air as he managed to get his 45 point blank with the Minotaur's remaining eye, then he squeezed the trigger.

Vegas wasn't sure how good the Minotaur's sense of smell was, so he immediately continued to attack with this sword before the monster could sniff out his position. In total darkness, the beast swung its remaining axe high and Vegas attacked, ready to end the contest of skill. Without landing on the ground and giving away his position, Vegas cut low, severing the beast's right leg, then its left arm. He then slit its throat, before finally boosting his sword's might with a surge of phoenix force before cutting the

Minotaur in half from bottom to top all in quick fluid motions. Vegas performed the attacks so fast, the Minotaur's body stayed intact. A heartbeat after his last strike, the Minotaur fell apart in puffs of blue energy and green blood.

When he saw the chunks of Minotaur on the ground, Vegas let himself relax as he turned to the blue doors and fell to both knees in exhaustion. He took note of his injuries and struggled to breathe normally. Only now did Vegas notice his heart practically beating out of his chest, his headache, dry mouth, ringing ears, and blurred vision. Vegas hung his head and looked over the rim of his glasses at the blue metal doors: at the entrance to unlimited power. Vegas allowed a gratifying smirk to etch his lips. After everything he had been through, after everything he had done and every monster he had to slay to get here, Vegas could only think of one thing appropriate to say at the precipice of this glorious moment.

"Mine."

* * * *

Before he could pull himself off the ground, Vegas heard Joe signaling that he wanted to talk over the earpiece. Vegas had muted Joe's end shortly before entering the long hallway the probes led him to. Using more strength then should have been necessary, Vegas reached and clicked on the earpiece.

"Vegas! Vegas we are in some serious deep shit!" Joe screamed franticly in Vegas' ear.

"Calm down," Vegas shouted back, "just tell me what's going on. We're almost done. All I have left is to get these doors open."

"Well, you better hurry! I'm pretty sure Miner is down 'cause the god particle machine is off line, and running off reserves now. You got twety minutes before you're smashed flatter than a skinny bitch's ass!"

"Twenty minutes should be enough time. What about Deep?"

"I haven't been able to contact him either! I think they both got taken out, and if Big O's, out then that means our ticket home is gone, too."

"Don't worry about it. I get this power and we'll get home, trust. I'll see if I can help Rob and Deep before we leave. Everything will be fine."

"Oh, well. Yeah, we have another problem."

"What?"

"What the hell is the Kiuper belt?" Joe asked.

"Whyyyyy?"

"Becaaaaaaause, the onboard computers have been going crazy about some crap from the 'Kiuper belt' moving in this direction."

"What! How long has the warning been going off?"

"I don't know, for a while now. You showed me how to fly and shoot the weapons on this thing. That's about it. I have no idea what the lights on this thing mean."

Vegas cursed himself. He had only taught Joe how to fly and fight in the ship if he had to. He was so focused on Jupiter and what he would find in the temple, Vegas didn't consider an attack like this—stupid! Vegas told Joe the sequence of buttons and switches he needed to hit to find out what was going on.

"Oh, fuck me sideways!" Joe yelped.

"What does it say?"

"It's saying that a bunch of really big rocks are going to hit Io, Europa, and Callisto and a warrior princess is going to smash into the temple."

"A warrior princess?"

"Yeah, you know Xena, warrior princess."

"Oh, shit! Shit!"

"What?"

"Xena is a dwarf planet in the Kiuper belt that's quite a bit larger than Pluto. Its name now is Eris after the Greek goddess of discord and strife, but I don't think the name change was made official. The Titans must have some way to hurl that stuff at us, but that doesn't make any sense."

"What doesn't make sense? Getting hit upside the head with a dwarf planet sounds like it would hurt to me."

"That's not the point. Jupiter has around sixty-five satellites orbiting it, most of them around the same size as Xena or bigger. Why wouldn't they try to crush us with one of them? It would be much faster and just as efficient—unless the moons of Jupiter do something to its orbit around the sun or has something to do with their power. Maybe the Titans' essence is locked away on the moons. Interesting."

"Wooooow, Vegas that is sooooo interesting—NOW WHAT THE FUCK DO WE DO ABOUT IT!?"

"We' aren't doing anything about it, but YOU are."

"Me?"

"Yes, you. You're going to have to use the ship and bust up those projectiles before they hit the temple. How much time do we have?"

"Eight minutes 'till Xena ninja kicks you in the head, and eighteen minutes before the reserves on the god particle machine fail. Even if I can stop these things, you're still screwed."

"Don't worry. All I have to do is get past these doors. I'll think of something. Now get going. I might need that extra ten minutes."

Joe sighed heavily into the headset. "All right. Good luck, Vegas."

"Same to you, buddy." Vegas said then disconnected the earpiece. There wouldn't be a reason to turn it back on. Vegas could tell that Joe understood that this was the all or nothing moment. If either one of them failed, they both would die. Vegas crushed, Joe stranded in space until the ship ran out of life support—they would win or they would die.

Vegas finally rose to his feet, his mind already trying to figure out how he would get through the blue metal doors and how he could use the remaining phoenix force to his advantage. Without warning, a surge of energy sparked to life as the massive machine in the back of the corridor kicked into overdrive.

Vegas was shocked when he thought he heard a low very evil and very powerful voice whisper, "My son is not finished yet, mortal."

"What the—"

Then Vegas turned and had to cover his eyes as the machine lit up like the sun. Fizzling energy reached out from the machine and grabbed the diced corpse of the Minotaur. Light and energy swirled around it until the body parts began to glow then lift off the ground. The light and energy grew and spun around faster and faster rising until it reached the top of the tall walls. As suddenly as it started the energy stopped, dispensing like a shattering light bulb, only to reveal a large Brahma bull made of glistening light! The bull was colossal in size, easily as tall as the dragon had been, and so wide it almost took up the entire width of the gigantic corridor. It stood strong and unyielding, chest proud and strong looking down on Vegas as if he were some filthy animal not worthy to touch him, let alone be in his presence.

The bull fixated on Vegas, its eyes burning with golden power and rage. Deep within those eyes, Vegas saw the same spark of intelligence mixed with the sharp sting of the previous defeat and intense longing for redemption. The bull rubbed its hoof against the ground causing deep groves in the ground as if preparing to charge. He then huffed deeply out its nostrils. Vegas pulled himself to his full height to stare back at the monster as gallantly and unafraid as his body would allow.

Seventeen minutes to defeat this bull, get through the seemingly impenetrable doors, and solve a mystery of how to unlock the potential energy beyond them. And that time would be cut in half if Joe wasn't able to stop the dwarf planet from crushing the temple. Vegas lips formed a half smile, half frown, as the bull lowered its head primed for attack, power pouring from it like heat from a burning tree.

"This is so fucked up."

Chapter 14

Joseph Warfield wasn't an engineer, or scientist, astronaut, genius, or a hero—super or regular, yet here he was alone in space at the controls of one of the most advanced vehicles he had ever seen on the Galilean moon, Callisto, with the universe on his shoulders.

"It's go time baby!" Joe said mustering up every ounce of focus and courage he could. He began flipping switches and pressing buttons initiating the ship's flight sequences. Joe also moved the countdown until meteor impact to the top of his view screen and the time the god particle machine had left on the bottom.

The ship sparked and hummed to life, and seconds later, Joe was raising high above Valhalla. Once he cleared the crater, Joe punched the accelerator then zoomed off into the darkness of space. Remembering everything Vegas had taught him, Joe switched the onboard viewing sensors to a different frequency, adjusted the thrusters and sights on the weapons. When he made the adjustments, he found the it wasn't just Xena, but a host of other smaller rocks flying alongside the dwarf planet.

It didn't take long for Joe to intercept the meteors. When they were in view, Joe took the controls and fired on the rocks. He couldn't hold back his grin as the first rock hit and blew into hundreds of pieces in all directions. At that point, Joe filled with confidence. He had the easy part, right? Just pilot the ship and blast shit outside—easy.

Wrong.

True, Joe was able to clear the smaller rocks quickly, but as he was powering up the main guns to ram Xena up the ass, the ship was attacked by something Joe couldn't see and the ships sensor couldn't pick up on. The ship tossed and turned as it was bumped off course. Lights and alarms went off like crazy.

"Computer! What's going on?" Joe shouted.

"Ship is under attack from various points thanks to pushing and pulling from external sources similar to dark matter," the ship's onboard computers replied. Joe had programmed the ship to sound like Beyoncé his newest celebrity crush. It seemed like a good idea at the time having Beyoncé to talk to while he was all alone on the ship, and as a matter of fact, it had been pretty sweet—until now. Sure the voice was sexy as hell, but not something you wanted to hear when you were about to be killed!

Joe was about to ask what the hell 'dark matter' was, but then he realized that he probably wouldn't understand the answer and wouldn't care.

"Ok, so what do I do about it?"

"Unknown. No real data about dark matter is available other than that it exists. Ships changes of survival—less than ten percent."

"Sweet!" Joe said sarcastically.

Joe fought with the controls with everything he had, but it was useless. The ship bounced back and forth like a bird caught in a tornado. There was a jolt to the ship that was so strong it rattled everything in the ship sending chills up through Joe's feet all the way to the crown of his head. The ship was supposed to have its own gravity, so the fact that Joe could feel the rumbling instead of just seeing it on the view screens was a very bad sign.

Turning to check on Vegas' body, Joe saw that some of the straps that held Vegas in place were coming undone. Joe switched the ship on autopilot, figuring it couldn't do any worse than he was, then ran to Vegas. Joe tried to repair the straps again. It was the fifth time Vegas had almost worked himself out of these things. Joe had to douse him with water three times to keep Vegas' temperature down. Somehow even though his body was physically on the ship; he still got several bruises and scratches on his body. Joe felt like a freaking nurse every the times he put ice on Vegas. It was also weird not seeing Vegas heal himself. Joe had always thought Vegas was unstoppable. Seeing him hurt like this, trying so hard when everything else seemed to come so easy, was the most unsettling thing about this whole trip for Joe.

Joe ran back to the controls determined to buy Vegas some time. If he couldn't fuck Xena, he could at least slap the bitch around some. Taking control of the targeting system, Joe converted half the ship's power to its weapons and the rest to life support. Selecting the weapon configuration he wanted and the time delays that felt right, Joe fired missiles and plasma energy blasts then launched a special surprise at Xena. Thankfully, Vegas had made the weapon controls as simple as point and click or Joe never would've been able to pull this off.

The first blast cleared the way as the other devices Joe launched reached near the dwarf planet's surface and exploded with the force of several hydrogen bombs. The shockwave, along with whatever else was pulling on the ship, sent the ship into a death spin into space.

As Joe drifted, he saw that Xena was still there but was knocked off course and slowing. Joe had no idea where he was in space and no idea if the ship would hold together. All he had was hope—hope that he had bought Vegas enough time to save everyone's ass!

Chapter 15

"You, my friend—are a goddamn cheater!" Vegas shouted as he narrowly dodged another attack from the golden bull's tremendous horns. The bull's grandiose persona dominated the large corridor and was only surpassed by its tenacious strength. The bull bucked, kicked, stomped and swung its horns, all in attempts to crash Vegas like an ant. Each time the bull made contact with the walls or floor its tremendous strength would send shockwaves rippling through them like a stone hitting a lake.

Vegas used his anti-gravitational shoes to stay away from any solid surface to avoid being pulverized by the shockwaves. As he dodged the attacks, his mind was running in overdrive filtering out his options. He was out of his heavy ordnance weapons, but since they didn't work on the dragon, there was no reason to believe they would work on this guy. Vegas' sword barely worked on the Minotaur before it went all super Saiyan so it was definitely out, and his optic exploding star beam was hard enough to use on Earth but using an avatar on Jupiter would be a one-trick pony at best. Vegas couldn't even attempt the optic blast again if he wanted and there was no way he could've survived it again anyway.

Deciding more information was necessary before making up his mind, Vegas knew he needed to take a risk. Vegas continued to evade the bull's blows. The impacts on the surrounding surfaces boomed louder than any thunder and generated forces greater than any explosion sending debris and energy flying everywhere. Sliding his hands together, Vegas commissioned his sword then used his glove to send the same crackling energy along its edges. Vegas still eluded the bull's attacks, but as he did, he positioned himself closer and closer to the golden beast. Eventually Vegas maneuvered himself right in front of the bull's eye. Using his sword, Vegas lunged at what he hoped would be a weak point in the bull's seemingly impenetrable hide.

Yet Vegas' theory didn't have the opportunity to be tested. Before he reached the bull's eye, Vegas heard an ominous cycling of energy followed by an intense glow where the bull's retina should have been if its eyes had not been solid light. Aborting his plan, Vegas used his shoes to propel himself upward just in time to avoid massive beams of force and light that came out in spirals from the bull's eyes. The force and power from the beast's eyes came out in a rush accompanied by a high pitch screech.

"WHAT—THE—FUCK?" Vegas shouted as he avoided beams of ostensibly concentrated sun light. This was not good. Vegas couldn't get too close to the bull or he would be crushed, and now he knew he couldn't get too far away or he would be laser-eyed to death. Perfect!

Vegas had one more special move up his sleeve, but he had no idea if it would work. The power source of his avatar had gotten a major boost from the phoenix. Vegas had run some calculations and had a working theory on how to use the extra power. But this was definitely a one-trick pony—no way the sun powering the avatar could be relit or re-energized after this. Vegas 'might' defeat the bull, but then he would have around five minutes to figure out how to unlock the power behind the blue doors.

Fuck it! Vegas thought. It wasn't like he had a lot of time anyway. Even if Joe managed to stop Xena, the god particle machine was still going to give out, crushing him instantly. If he was going to go out Vegas was going out swinging. As he darted between narrowly missing strikes of the bull Vegas ran angles, mathematic formulas, and equations through his mind until he felt he was ready.

Slapping his hands together, then hitting his left hand to his chest, Vegas tapped into the phoenix force, changed the reactions of the sun's core that was powering his avatar causing the sun to evolve from a yellow sun into a red giant. The energy and size of the red giant grew, pushing the avatar to its limits. The red sun grew so much that Vegas could feel it pushing against the walls of the sun's chamber. The power was too much to contain in the avatar alone, so Vegas had to re-channel it. The result was crimson fizzling power pulsing from Vegas' eyes like some unnatural dynamo. The reaction didn't increase Vegas' strength, speed, or agility, but with some additional configurations, it did let Vegas set his plan into motion.

If the bull noticed the change in Vegas, it ignored it and continued its unencumbered assault. Immediately Vegas put his plan in motion, before the avatar had time to burn out. Vegas slapped his hands together this time, accidentally creating sparks of lightning followed by burning ozone and thunder. Then as the bull tried to ram him with its head, as he had numerous times before, Vegas held his ground. Taking his left hand that now hummed and sparked with excess power, Vegas created a large circle of energy in front of himself using a clockwise motion. When the circle was complete, it left behind a thin barrier of energy. The bull's head collided with his would-be force field shattering it like tissue paper. Then Vegas jumped with all his might and twisted in the air until he was looking down on the top of the bull's head.

Again using a clockwise motion, Vegas created another wall of energy; the bull bucked upward again shattering the energy field. This time Vegas parried right avoiding the golden bull's body. Creating another field, Vegas waited for the beast to find him. When it found him, it tried to impale Vegas with one of its horns only dismembering another shield instead as Vegas swan dived out of the way. Vegas repeated this process over and over. Each time he did it, the walls of energy took a fraction of a second longer to break.

In retrospect, nothing had changed since the golden bull appeared. It was still attacking like a savage beast and Vegas was still barely avoiding death with every move it made. The only thing Vegas was thankful for was that the bull didn't have the awareness and foresight like the Minotaur had as he originally thought. If it did, Vegas was certain this plan wouldn't work.

The pace of the fighting picked up as the bull got more frustrated continuingly smashing the fields Vegas was putting up. Finally the bull rammed one of the energy fields and stumbled back like it hit a stone wall, instead of a glass window. It advanced again this time bursting through the field with added force. When Vegas saw that, he felt confident enough to try the next step.

Vegas bobbed then weaved into the angles he wanted and threw up another field. This one also stopped the bull short. This time Vegas used the opportunity to put some distance between himself and the bull. As he expected, the bull maintained its onslaught with beams of energy from its eyes. Vegas kept dodging using the fields until they were powerful enough to resist the bull's distant attack. Then Vegas charged at the bull, sprinting with everything he had holding a scarlet wall of energy in front of him as he advanced.

The bull shot its beams at Vegas, but they bounced off creating sparks and colors like paint being thrown at a wall. Its attack being deflected so easily wasn't going over well with the bull as its golden frame began to shine brighter, then it roared like a demon anxious for blood and the quick death of its enemy. The beaming power increased and Vegas felt his shield cracking. He disengaged the power in his shoes letting himself fall back head-first tucking himself into a ball and letting his momentum carry him forward just as the shield broke. He flipped until he was running on air again then tossed up another shield. The bull adjusted, its beams pushed upward in a rainbow of colors as Vegas' shield grew stronger. Once again the bull roared, increasing its power. Vegas jumped doing a front flip over the shield as it shattered, then pushed forward throwing up another shield. When the bull adjusted, he smashed that shield Vegas summoned, causing him to conjured another shield. This time the beams were forced downward as he advanced.

"I wish you were smart enough to realize that these shields have been absorbing the power of your attacks!" Vegas shouted as he neared the bull. "It would make my question sweeter if you answered, but I still have to ask."

Vegas spun to his right as he reached the shining bull, but with one quick jab step left, he was at the beast's right jaw. As it turned to attack, Vegas' left hand burst into a brilliant humming crimson energy. "Why ya hitting yourself!" Vegas barked as his left fist connected with the side of the bull's face, hammering it with all the built up kinetic energy, driving it into the opposite wall.

The power of the punch was so great it stunned the bull and created an enormous crack in the wall. Vegas backed up, clapped his hands together then waved his hands from side to side letting the energy trail he created stabilize until he was holding two long energy strands. He twirled the energy whips in a display occasionally cracking the whips, breaking the sound barrier, all to get the bull's attention.

Obviously, still dazed from Vegas' punch, the bull hobbled to its feet. Vegas began cracking the whips across the bull's head, mouth and eyes, throwing it off balance. Then

Vegas wrapped one whip around the bull's horns and another around one of its legs. He tugged and yanked until the bull was right where he wanted it. The bull tried to fight back, but Vegas positioned it so that it wouldn't have any leverage. With one sharp blow to the top of the head, the bull's head slammed to the ground and its front end bounced like it landed on a trampoline rather that a rock hard floor. Vegas twisted until he was under the bull then punched it again while it was in the air. Modifying the whips, Vegas drove them deep into the ground then concentrated all the remaining power from the red giant core into one last punch. The power in Vegas' fist was so intense he was worried his hand would shatter. It pulsated a bright red, sending sparks and waves of energy with every move.

Vegas unloaded a thunderous haymaker straight into the bull's chest cavity sending it flying into the blue metal doors. When the bull impacted the door they both exploded and created a magnificent light display, greater than any fireworks. Vegas had to look away blocking the light with his arms while his legs struggled to stand firm as if Vegas were in the middle of hurricane winds.

When the winds stopped, Vegas turned to look and saw the blue metal doors as well as the bull were gone. Vegas could see a box sitting on top of an altar shining with a rainbow of colors—the most beautiful thing he had ever seen.

"All mine." Vegas said, and then walked toward his well-earned prize.

* * * *

Vegas summoned a dagger using his glove in case he had to pry the box open, but before he could reach the entrance to the power, his anti-gravitational shoes gave out and he fell to the ground with a thud. The energy of the red giant had all been siphoned off; Vegas knew that meant only a white dwarf was now left in its place. The expansion and power of the red giant had burned away all the fuel Vegas had in the avatar's core, and the white dwarf could barely generate the power to perform the operations needed to move against Jupiter's gravity.

Checking the time, Vegas saw he had eleven minutes before the god particle machine's power reserves were drained away. Vegas somehow found the energy to bring his hands together. The energy in his glove popped weakly. Vegas placed his hand on his chest and closed his eyes. His only hope was to manipulate the avatar to maximize the power of the white dwarf. Changing the power couplings for the avatar was risky; one wrong configuration would render it useless, but Vegas didn't have a choice. It took almost a full minute, but Vegas was able to get the avatar to use the extremely high density of the star to his advantage. It took another thirty seconds for the power to build high enough for Vegas to move somewhat normally again.

Pulling himself to his feet, Vegas limped toward the box of energy leaving him one minute to figure out how to release the power if Joe wasn't able to stop Xena. The box was much bigger than Vegas had originally thought. It was more of a coffin than a box. Vegas scanned the coffin with his eyes searching for any traps or levers, places for a key, anything. It looked oddly simple—just push the lid off. So Vegas inserted his dagger into the crack where the lid met the coffin. He used the dagger as a fulcrum, and to his surprise, the lid popped off. When it came off so easily, Vegas jumped back in anticipation of—well, of something. If his time in the Titan's temple had taught him anything, it was that there was always a bomb or an ambush just around the corner. Yet nothing jumped out and attacked Vegas, nothing blew up; it was very weird and uncharacteristic of the other chambers in the temple.

"You're destine to die mortal!" the same infamous deep growling voice that spoke before the Minotaur was transformed spoke from off in the distance. The voice came from the opposite side where the machine at the far end of the corridor stood. Vegas spun his dagger, raised it ready to fight, even though he could barely move; let alone defend himself.

"Who said that? Show yourself," Vegas demanded but no one and nothing appeared.

"You are doomed. You are too weak to control what you seek."

Vegas peered into the long dark hallway where the machine at the far end lit up and dimmed like it was breathing.

Focus Vegas, Joe much have stopped Xena so you got six minutes. Don't let some ghost voice distract you.

Vegas turned back to the coffin, pushed the lid completely off, and found the last thing he expected.

"You got to be shit'n me." Vegas deadpanned as he examined the contents of the coffin. There wasn't any power that he could see, no puzzle, no all powerful sword, no indestructible armor, no goblet of power giving elixir, not even a magical cube, only the weirdest animal Vegas had ever seen in his life. Whatever it was swam in water that filled the coffin, its back end looked like a serpent and its front resembled—a cow. The cow part had sad blue eyes and black fur with patches of white. The creature's black fur seemed to melt into its brown and black lower reptilian half that was slimy looking similar to an overgrown eel. "Mmmmooooo," the creature said looking at Vegas with its sad, childlike eyes.

"Bullshit—what the fuck is this?" At that second, Vegas was angrier than he had ever been in his life. He couldn't believe he had come so far, risked so much to find—this! Whatever this was. Plus he had less than five minutes before he would be crushed by Jupiter's atmospheric pressure.

Ok, calm down. You knew whatever the power was it registered as potential energy. This thing has to be it, just need to figure this out.

But Vegas didn't have a clue what to do. The creature swam up to Vegas and tenderly licked his hand like a dog showing affection for its owner. Vegas couldn't help think the thing was—cute. For some reason its innocence was calming; you couldn't help wanting to take care of the damn thing.

"You see mortal, you are lost—you have lost!"

"Shut up!" Vegas spat.

"Soon you will be crushed into nothingness by our weapon of choice."

"Stop talking! Whoever you are, you will be crushed, too!"

"We are immortal. We cannot die, only removed from this realm, but we will always rise again."

"Shut! Up!"

"The eternal power of Titanomachia was never yours to hold. Prepare for your death." The voice laughed before trailing off, retreating back into the darkness. Then—it all clicked for Vegas when he had three minutes left to live, plenty of time. The voice probably didn't intend to, but he had told Vegas everything he needed to know to unlock this power and save the universe—and more importantly himself!

Then without warning, the entire temple started to shake abruptly. There was a loud cacophony that came from every direction. If the god particle machine had failed; Vegas would've been crushed instantly. This shaking could only mean that Joe only managed to slowdown Xena but not stop it entirely.

Vegas grabbed the serpent bull by the throat, and then turned it on its back exposing its soft belly. The serpent-bull shrieked in terror and pain as Vegas used his dagger to cut into the harmless creature and then pull its entrails out flopping them on the ground in front of the coffin.

Judging from the shaking and sounds, Vegas estimated he had fifty seconds before the dwarf planet hit the temple. Vegas reached into the carcass of the creature trying to gather all of its internal organs. Then he dumped them on the ground in front of the coffin.

As quickly as he could with the temple trembling around him, Vegas piled all the innards together then looked around for anything he could use to start a fire.

Thirty seconds left.

Of course, they wouldn't have anything to start a fire in here. If Vegas couldn't start a fire, he couldn't unlock the power he needed. Frantically, he searched his mind trying to figure out what he could do. Vegas knew he had to set this pile of guts on fire, but how?

Twenty seconds left.

After everything, it ends here. Looking at the power he needed, it seemed so close yet so far away! He thought everything through and reached his goal. Vegas had proven he was inimitable, had done the impossible, yet he was about to die because he didn't pack a fucking lighter. Then, Vegas remembered his battle with the dragon.

Ten seconds.

The sound increased and echoed as Xena made contact with the top of the temple. Vegas could actually feel the temple giving way as billions of tons of rock and debris rushed to meet him. Vegas spent a lot of time figuring out how to make the orbs of light without fire, but the flammable orbs had been easy to make. Remembering the formula he used to light the way around the combustible lake, Vegas took a deep breath focusing ever last bit of the avatar's strength to this one final task. Vegas snapped his fingers creating a ball of flame, then the chamber around him collapsed plunging Vegas into what he thought was an eternal darkness. Yet at that point, Vegas felt that everything made sense.

Chapter 16

Joe knew he was still alive, but he didn't really know how. He felt like he had been continuously hit upside the head with a baseball bat. At least one of his ribs had to be broken as well as his left leg. The ship's life support systems had all started to fail and there were multiple hull breaches all throughout the ship when Joe lost consciousness, so how was he still alive?

Joe struggled to his feet using the ship's consoles for support and then tried to see how badly the ship was damaged. A feeling of despair came over Joe as he realized that even though he had survived the blast, he was still doomed. Tears slowly washed over his cheeks as he wished that he would've died when he set the bombs off. He thought instant death would've been better than sitting in a cold dark spacecraft waiting to suffocate.

This was Joe's big chance to escape his boring mundane life. Joe had wanted to make his life matter, he wanted to make a difference, but it was all for nothing. He wouldn't have been upset about dying if he knew the universe was safe, but it wasn't. Vegas' body lay in a heap covered in broken machines and support beams. Rob and Deep were likely killed—their bodies floating aimlessly through space just as Joe soon would be, and it was all for nothing.

Looking around, Joe found a sharp piece of shrapnel and picked it up in his good hand. Joe didn't have the patience to sit around to wait and die. He wasn't going to let his mind drift off into insanity and desperation during his last moments. He was alone. A billion miles away from another person with zero chance of rescue, Joe was going to go out on his terms and no other way.

Lifting the shrapnel high, Joe prepared to cut open his belly spilling his guts on the floor ending his life before insanity could tug at him any longer. He took several deep breaths until he was finally ready, his hands steady and determined and then—a magnificent light appeared from where Vegas' body lay.

The debris around Vegas dissolved almost like it had melted away, but more like it was forced into nonexistence. The crimson light grew and grew causing Joe to drop his suicide weapon to cover his eyes. The light was warm and piercing as if it were shining through Joe, rather than reflecting on him. Just as quickly as it came, the light dimmed. Joe looked at the source of radiance, his eyes squinting desperately trying to make out the figure that stood before him like a human light bulb.

"You weren't about to give up were you?" Joe heard a familiar voice ask from the brightness.

"Vegas?"

"None other," Vegas said stepping forward turning down the light show.

"Dude—why are you naked again?" Joe remarked. Even when the light was lowered enough for Joe to see, Vegas still had a ghostly scarlet glow about him. Vegas had always been in good shape, but now his muscles were bigger and more defined. You could see each muscle bulging even with the slightest move. His body was covered in red light and bursts of white star-light that appeared all over Vegas as if he were a living scarlet night sky. Joe couldn't tell if Vegas was breathing, but everything around him was pushed and contracted as though Vegas' presence was making everything more vibrant. There was a slight hum coming from Vegas; power was cycling though Vegas' body that he couldn't fully control. The most unsettling thing Joe noticed was Vegas' eyes. They were dead, devoid of any real emotion. Seemingly any trace of connection to humanity had been washed away replaced with power beyond Joe's understanding.

Joe watched as Vegas inspected his new body, looking from his hands, to his chest and down. Then Vegas found a reflective piece of metal on the floor that seemed to hold his attention as he stared at his own reflection.

"Vegas?" Joe asked trying to pull Vegas away from the image of himself. "Oh, captain, my captain? Vegas, you in there man?"

"I'm here, Joe. It's just—it's a big change to get used to it all."

Joe was relieved that while Vegas looked different, he still sounded the same. "How do you feel?"

"I feel like—like I've discovered an extra emotion. As if I—I'm able to see what was always in front of me. Everything seems so clear now, as if nothing is above my ability to comprehend, like the universe holds no mysteries from me."

"Why don't you seem more excited? It worked! You have powers—you're a glowing red bad-ass mother fucker! You can totally kick Gor's ass now. You've always wanted powers and now you got them. Everything is going to be better now right—right?"

Joe watched Vegas as he pulled himself from his own reflection. For a brief moment, Joe noticed a sadness he had never witnessed in Vegas. It was like Vegas had lost something very important to him.

"Vegas?"

"There is still much to do," Vegas said more to himself than Joe. Vegas closed his eyes then extended his arms outward palms up. After a brief moment, his hands started to glow followed by the entire ship. At an unbelievable speed, the ship began to piece itself back together. Support beams were put back in place, wires restored, weldings restored, dents pushed out, and then the ship was made better than it was before.

Before he could comment, Joe felt something cover him. It was as if a blanket made of warm light was pulled over his body; after that, it felt like a sensation of energy was gently raining down on him. When it stopped, Joe's ribs didn't ache, his leg could move pain free and his head stopped throbbing. He was completely healed!

"Sweet!" Joe shouted.

"Take the ship and get it back in Jupiter's orbit. I'll meet you there."

"On it, but what's the plan? Shouldn't you be heading to the center of the galaxy and whatnot?"

"First, I have to try to save Rob and Deep."

"They're still alive? How do you know?"

"I don't. But I have faith in their tenacity. I have to try."

"Right, then you're off to stomp a mud hole in Gor right?"

"Wrong."

"Wrong—why wrong?"

"The Titans never intended for me to be killed by Xena. It was just an elaborate ruse. It just would've been an added bonus to them as they released something almost as terrible as Gor on the galaxy. Before I can deal with Gor, I must handle this new treat."

"What new—" but before Joe could finish his question, Vegas disappeared in a flash of crimson. Even with all his powers and new found awareness, Vegas still had a way to pop your bubble of relief. As soon as you thought things were getting better—they got ten times worse.

* * * *

Robert Holley had done everything that he could possibly do, but it wasn't enough. He had fought with everything he had, pushed his powers to the limit, but it just wasn't good enough. The worst part was that Rob was actually winning. Even while going berserk, Rob had managed to keep his head straight enough to create a fortified position. The molten army could only attack him from one direction. For a while they were nothing more than lambs to the slaughter, as Rob bashed all that threatened the god particle machine.

Even the giant rock creature fell to Rob, as he busted its ankles causing it to fall taking out thousands of its allies. Rob had found a nice flow to the battle and momentum was in his favor, until rocks started falling from space. Without warning or sound, asteroids hit the god particle machine rendering it useless in seconds. He survived the asteroid barrage, but he had been devastated. He knew what that machine meant to the survival of the universe, to saving his wife.

With the machine gone, Rob had no reason to hold back, no reason for caution, and was no longer fighting handicapped. Since he didn't need to power the machine, he unleashed his full wrath on the molten arm. He screamed like a mad man with nothing to lose, charging with no thought of his own safety, the destruction of the enemy his only aim. The ferocity of Rob's attacks grew and grew, but the enemy kept coming. For every one molten man Rob crushed, ten more would take its place! Rob had lost all sense of self as he failed wildly. Finally his powers grew to an unprecedented scale. Each attack he delivered affected the entire moon of Io.

If Io was going to keep coughing up these fucking things, then Rob was going to destroy Io itself! Rob had long since stopped thinking. He didn't consider the consequences of destroying Io with him still on it, and he didn't think about the fact that he may not be powerful enough to accomplish it. He was running on pure instinct when he reached his axe high into the air, screamed something that wasn't exactly English, then hit the ground creating a massive shockwave that rippled through the moon cracking all the way down to its core. The crack extended in different directions that ran along the entire surface of the moon.

With its core so badly compromised, all the pressure, lava, and trapped gas gushed out of the moon like air out of a balloon. The molten army all collapsed because Io no longer had the energy to sustain them; The whole moon shook tremendously as an enormous amount of energy and debris was shot from the moon into space. The blast came from the opposite side of the moon, but it was so powerful it sent Io slightly closer to Jupiter. Not much, but enough that the gas giant's gravity had finally entrenched Io into its death grip. Now, it was only a matter of time before Jupiter opened wide and swallowed the moon by tearing it into pieces.

Rob had a good enough grip on the moon that he hadn't been blown away from the shockwave that the dying moon's core had produced. Rob was beyond exhaustion as he lay on a floating chunk of Io. The moon was slowly dissolved into Jupiter and began to burn up in its atmosphere. Rob was tired; it even felt like he had to put effort into keeping his heart pumping. Rob noticed his axe was broken and drifting above his head just out of his reach, the P.A.G, Vegas had made to keep him alive in space, was cracked and flashing wildly—that was when Rob knew it was over.

He looked up at Jupiter one last time, hating the big ball of gas with everything he had left to hate within him. Rob stuck his middle finger at the planet for one final "fuck you" then he was ready to let go and die.

Just as Rob took what he knew would be his last breath; he saw a bright light glowing in front of him. The light was warm and healing, making every worry Rob ever had go away. It was like whatever he had to do could wait—or rather that someone else would take care of it. He tried to reach for the light, but didn't have the strength. Satisfied that he had done all he could do and given everything he had to give, Rob felt himself being lifted towards the light as a hand reached down to claim him.

Funny, Rob thought. *I never would'a thought the light to heaven would be so—red.*

* * * *

Deep Willis—was in deep shit. He had no idea what he was going to do or how he was going to redeem himself. The worst part was that he was cut off from Vegas and the others, so he had no idea if anything he did even mattered. Had Vegas found the power and abandoned everyone? Had Rob failed to keep the god particle machine going long enough for Vegas to even get the power? Was Vegas dead, killed by one of the many Greek giants in the temple? Deep had no way of knowing, so he decided he shouldn't care.

He had no idea how long it had been since the Hydra forced him into the icy dark oceans of Europa, but it felt like it had been days! The Hydra had attacked too many times to count, but for now it was content to leave Deep to drift among the black seemingly bottomless waters. When he was first plunged in the waters, Deep searched for the generators he had been trying to refuel. He had managed to fight off the Hydra and find the generators once, but only because the Hydra had been toying with him. Once he lost sight of the space fold generators a second time, Deep knew he had no hope of ever finding them again. The Hydra was smarter than it looked. He had fought Deep into the direction of the generators only to drag him away again. There was no way it was pure coincidence; the Hydra must have done it on purpose. Now it continued to attack Deep every so often like a dog pouncing its favorite chew toy.

Deep had wanted to avoid the cold darkness of space, but this was just as bad if not worse. He had no sense of direction and no hope of escaping his adversary. The only thing that stopped him from reverting back to his human form and letting the pressure of Europa's water kill him instantly was the hate he felt for the Hydra and the slim hope for revenge he held on to with all he had. If Deep had been on solid land with the amount of strength he had now, the Hydra would've been dead in seconds, but floating in water where he had no leverage, his strength counted for almost nothing.

The Hydra had also figured out how Deep's body worked. Now instead of trying to swallow him whole or bite off one of his limbs, the Hydra was using its heads to attack simultaneously from many different angles. Each attack was meant to pull Deep in different directions in an attempt to rip him apart—and it almost worked several times. Deep had sensations he had never felt before when he was Obsidian: feelings like his shoulder was pulled out of its socket, his leg dislocated, and his spine pulled out of alignment. Thankfully his Obsidian body healed and the sensations went away between attacks, but the attacks had grown more and more effective and each time his pain became more intense.

Deep's mind tried to formulate a plan, but it was nearly impossible to think of anything he could do when the Hydra could defy the laws of physics. Roaring in space was one thing, but no sound when the Hydra attacked under water? The vibrations from its movements should have registered as some form of sound, but nothing but spikes of pain had signaled the Hydra's arrival.

Deep resented every moment of torture at the jaws of this beast! In between attacks, Deep thought of his life—what he had done wrong and what he had done right. He thought of his days as a professional mixed-martial arts fighter and his time at his current job as a geology professor at UNLV. There was so much more Deep wanted to do before he died—so much more he wanted to accomplish and teach. There were lives he wanted to touch.

Like a hungry viper, the Hydra attacked again. It was a lengthier attack compared to the others, and this time almost succeeded in ripping Deep apart. When the Hydra retreated and Deep healed, he felt himself tittering on the edge of sanity. Deep may die in the bowels of Europa, but he was going to make sure the Hydra's rotting carcass would join his.

Finally, Deep had a plan. It wasn't something that he would normally do, not his normal style, but he didn't have any other choice. Normally Deep preferred to have all the information and parameters at hand before he would consider putting a plan into action, but now wasn't the time to be picky. Without knowing if he was facing the right direction, Deep turned then clapped his hands together with all his strength. The clap created a big boom followed by and a small light was sparked then quickly snuffed out and Deep was propelled in the opposite direction. Deep preformed the move again, then again. Finally through sheer luck, he hit a solid surface.

Deep felt what he had hit and when he was confident it wasn't just a piece of ice but a solid core, he dug his hand into the ground and kneeled, waiting for the Hydra's next attack—if it would dare attack him now.

Come on you nine headed bastard—come on! Deep thought as he kneeled in wait for his tormentor to assault him again. Finally it came. This time when the Hydra silently grabbed Deep, he used the ground to anchor himself long enough to grab the neck of one of the heads. Using the ground as leverage, Deep twisted flipping the Hydra over his shoulder onto the murky ocean bottom.

Before the Hydra could regain its composure, Deep took hold of the neck right below the head and proceeded to spin the monster over his head like an ancient warrior priming a slingshot. Deep was spinning the monster so hard and so fast, he had to bend and hold the ground with his three powerful fingers to keep from being blown back into the depths of the unforgiving ocean.

Then when the spinning reached maximum velocity, Deep used every ounce of muscle he had and every bit of leverage he could muster to slam the Hydra into the ocean floor. This time Deep felt the ocean move as if he were standing in a giant fish bowl someone was tapping on. Deep heard the sound of the ground buckle and crack then felt a pull as water rushed to fill the crack. The Hydra had gone limp in Deep's hands, so he used the chance to end this before it regained conscious. Running his hands along the Hydra's body, Deep finally reached its rear end where he clutched each of the monsters' hind legs in his hands.

Let's see you regrow this!

Deep extended his arms, working his way up to the Hydra's heads, as he split the monster in half from the bottom up. Deep could feel the monsters' heads move in panic as it pushed the water back and forth which meant that it was now alive and conscious to feel itself being ripped apart—*Good,* Deep thought.

The flailing stopped when Deep reach the Hydra's necks severing them from the body. Deep's only regret was that he couldn't see the Hydra as he killed it, that he couldn't see it experience the pain he inflicted.

Now that he was triumphant, Deep let himself fall to the ocean floor and let himself give in to the moon's gravity. Of course, Deep had realized that he could have used the

Hydra to propel himself to the surface, but what good would that have done? He'd only be exchanging one dark endless void for another.

Feeling that he had somewhat redeemed himself by killing the Hydra, Deep closed his eyes and then began to let himself revert back to his human form. Slowly the coldness grew and the pressure pushed down harder on Deep until it would eventually crush his body. With his eyes closed, Deep felt life drain away when a gorgeous red light painted the darkness and Deep let himself go into the great beyond.

* * * *

Vegas was standing back on the ship that he had fixed using only the power of his mind with friends he had willed to full health, yet he was struggling to understand his emotions. As much as he wanted to understand how he felt, he also didn't care. He didn't care about anything—why was that?

"Dude! Can you please put some clothes on?" Joe screamed as Vegas appeared still glowing like an evil Christmas tree with Rob and Deep standing beside him.

Vegas ignored Joe's comment and turned his attention to Rob and Deep.

"Are you two all right?" Vegas asked.

"Wo,wo,wo!" Rob said as he inspected his body and then the axe in his hand. "How am I still alive? How is my axe put back together? What da hell just happened?"

Deep remained silent as if taking in everything around him and trying to put the pieces together on his own.

"We have accomplished our goals, my friends. I was able to obtain the power the Titans held guarded in the center of their temple."

"Vegas? Is that you? Why are ya glow'n like a human stop light?" Rob asked and both Deep and Joe turned to Vegas waiting for an answer.

"Very well, I believe you all are deserving of an explanation as to what has transpired. The power that the Titans were guarding was the Ophiotaurus."

"Holy shit!" Rob exclaimed. "Are ya serious? I never even woulda thought of that."

"We're very happy for you, Miner, since you already know what the hell an Ophitarasaurs or whatever the hell it's called, but could you please let Mr. Lava lamp here explain it?" Joe asked.

"The correct name is O-phio-taurus, Joseph," Deep corrected as he looked like he was starting to put everything together. "Please, Vegas, go on."

"The Ophiotaurus is a creature that only appeared once in Greek myth. It was an innocent harmless creature and it was said that if someone was to cut it open and set fire to its entrails, that person would gain limitless power, enough to topple the reign of the gods and bring them to their knees. The Titans—Kronus, Koios, Krios, Iapetos, Hyperion, and Okeanos—had planned for one of their servants to slay the creature to use its power during the Titanomachia. However, Zeus sent an eagle to snatch the entrails before they could be cast into the fire. The Ophiotaurus was never heard from again, until I found it locked away in the temple."

"What now?" Deep asked.

"Now I have an unexpected urgent matter to attend—observe." Vegas waved his hand and the hull of the ship became transparent allowing everyone to see Jupiter in all its newfound horror. Instead of its normal patterns of multi-colored swirling storms and wind patterns, the entire planet had been transformed into one humongous storm system. All the layered bands had merged together; massive lightning grew so powerful it shot out of the planet's atmosphere into space, and as if that weren't bad enough, the planet seemed to actually be growing.

"Bohica." Rob deadpanned.

"Indeed," Vegas replied.

"Lightning shooting from the planet into space, the energy needed to create a storm system on that scale—it's scientifically impossible," Deep remarked.

"This is not science as you know it at work, my friend," Vegas answered. "This is a power we have never seen. The Titan-god Typhon has been unleashed."

"Holy horse shit!" Rob exclaimed.

"Can you defeat it?" Deep asked.

"I am unsure of the full force of the power I have acquired. The legend said that the power of the Ophiotaurus was meant to destroy Zeus and the other Olympian gods. The power was never unleashed, so there is no way to know exactly what I can do now. I am forced to make this up as I go."

"What do we even know about this Typhoon mother fucker?" Joe inquired. "Can't we just leave him for later? We still have Gor to deal with and we know he's a major bad ass. Shouldn't you focus on him?"

"Typhon was a real heavy hitter in Greek myth's kid. The gods barely defeated'em. It was more luck than anything else—if I remember da story right. Typhon had beaten Zeus but his arrogance gave Zeus a chance ta recover, then he beat Typhon when he wasn't expecting it."

"Correct, Rob, but there are things that had been left out of the myths. Once the gods and Titans fell in to the myths and legends of humans, they withdrew from Earth. Then Zeus still had some control over the Titans and was able to imprison them on Jupiter and its surrounding moons, since the planet represented his power in Roman times.

"Putting a power like the Ophiotaurus in place alongside the Titans, knowing they could never use it, is the type of punishment a god like Zeus would've enjoyed. Typhon's power is so enormous it cannot be fully contained, which was evident by the great red spot. Over the centuries the great red spot has been reduced by half. At first I thought Typhon's power was being drained away, but now I see that it was all part of his plan to escape by crushing the temple. He had tried with a comet that humans called shoemaker levy 9, but he couldn't penetrate deep enough into the planet to hit the temple. However the god particle machine gave Typhon the perfect opportunity to free himself. Now unless I stop him, he will free the other Titans and return to Earth. The gods are too weak to stop him and with no warning, there would be nothing that could stop them."

"That's some bad shit and all, but what about Gor? This storm monster may threaten Earth, but Gor is gonna butt fuck the whole damn universe if we don't stop him."

"Joseph does have a point, Vegas," Deep recanted.

"No!" Rob insisted. "We have ta stop Typhon from free'n the other Titans and reaching Earth. If we don't, it wouldn't matter what Gor does if our home is taken over by the Titans."

"I agree with all of your concerns, but there is only one course of action I can take at this point," Vegas said as he started to glow brighter red and levitate. "I must attempt to defeat both Typhon and then Gor."

Everyone turned from Vegas back to Jupiter as the planet shot out more massive amounts of lightning in all directions with cones of gas and wind swirling, extending from the planet.

"It's too late for that now, look! If you take on this thing now, you might not have enough to handle Gor. Maybe if you didn't float here yap'n and explaining stuff, you could've beat him easy when he first got out."

"Typhon's power hasn't grown, Joe, only his level of intimidation. His full power was set loose when Xena obliterated the temple and the chamber that held him." Vegas retorted, "Besides, if I cannot defeat Typhon who threatens our planet, I would have no hope of defeating Gor who seeks destruction on a much greater scale and possesses much more power. My lack of knowledge in my new power shouldn't inspire a lack of confidence in them. The Chosen One of Legend led me here for a reason—I believe Typhon is to be my warm up."

"Goddamn! Typhon—a warm up. Buddy, if that's the case then you one badass mo'fo right now that's for sure," Rob stated.

"Ok, fine! Nobody listen to me, I'm just the little guy with no power that flies the ship. What do I know, right? We could go warn the other heroes on Earth and they can hold off Typhon until Vegas gets back but whatever—whatever!"

"Calm down, Joseph! This is Vegas' call," Deep insisted then looked to Vegas and the others followed his lead.

Vegas effortlessly hung in the air, but an incredible burden seemed to hang on his shoulders. After seconds of contemplations, Vegas had confidently made his decision.

"The three of you take the ship and make your way back to Earth. When you get there, alert Panda Jack, Jen, and any other heroes you can contact and alert them to the possible threat. Leave several probes behind to monitor the battle and to convince anyone that may be doubtful. However, I'm sure the metamorphosis of Jupiter is visible from Earth through telescopes."

Suddenly something portentous and alarming shifted in Vegas' eyes. "Yes—yes, that's it. I see it now," Vegas said as he stared at Jupiter with a type of lust growing in his eyes. "All of you go home, and forget alerting anyone else Joe. I will be victorious. I understand. Not even the Chosen One could defeat me as I am now."

Without another word Vegas disappeared with a hum of power and a flash of light. Vegas was gone leaving only the ominous echoing laugh of a man drunk with power.

"Well, he seemed different there at da end," Rob said expressionless.

The remaining trio didn't speak for several moments because there simply wasn't anything to say. A common unspoken consensus passed between them. As happy as they were to find out that Vegas had been telling the truth the whole time, the weight of reality pushed even harder on all of them. Plus they knew how Vegas could be—could he be trusted with such power? What would happen if he were successful and defeated Gor? Each of the remaining heroes couldn't help but wonder—had they just helped unleash something potentially more dangerous than Gor ever was?

Chapter 17

Jen was in his apartment above his record store doing his nightly meditation exercise. He sat in a cross-legged position surrounded by different scented candles. As he breathed in the sweet aromas, the flames would dim. As he breathed out, they would intensify. It was a simple exercise to keep his circulation of Chi in balance and something that he looked forward to each night. It was the only thing, besides music, that gave him a sense of peace and helped him find his center.

This was normally a calm undisturbed time for Jen until a surprising burst of crimson light appeared in front of him. At first Jen thought it was the Chosen One of Legend, but then the power emanating from the light was much different than anything Jen had ever felt the Chosen One give off. Whereas Chosen One's energy had always radiated a positive and reassuring essence, this power was much more—dubious. Though non-threatening, it had a measure of duplicity that couldn't be fully hidden. This told Jen the hint of malice was either intentional or the work of a novice.

Regardless, Jen remained seated but primed himself for whatever might transpire. Jen's energy built until his skin gave off a slight golden glow. Within seconds, the silhouette of a man formed and out of the light, Vegas stepped forward. This, however, wasn't Vegas as Jen had last seen him. Now his skin was shining red and brilliant sparks of light like stars were emanating from all over his body, his muscles were more toned and formed, his eyes gleamed like crimson suns, and he appeared completely naked as if the concept of clothing was foreign to him. Even when he recognized who it was stepping though the light, Jen still didn't relax his guard or diminish his golden aura.

"Hello, Vegas," Jen said with a slight smile as he nodded his head in respect.

"Jen," Vegas replied returning the gesture.

"It appears you were telling the truth about the power on Jupiter—and that you were successful in acquiring it."

"Of course, I was telling the truth, and yes, the guarded power of the Titans is now mine."

"You have already defeated your adversary?"

"I only just received this power."

"Then I would assume you would be battling Gor—to what do I owe the pleasure of your visit?"

"Gor is still a threat, but there is time to spare. At the moment, there is a more pressing concern on which I want to seek your council."

"Go on."

Jen sat and listened patiently for five minutes as Vegas recanted the events that had allowed him to acquire his new-found power. The story was uncharacteristic in its detail, but more than that Jen noticed Vegas' body language, his inflections, how he strung his words and thoughts together. Everything about Vegas seemed to shift in and out from his normal self to a state of enlightenment. Also Vegas' aura pulsed like a heartbeat; power was constantly dripping from him. Jen thought of it like a water faucet that couldn't be closed all the way. Even though Jen knew the threat of Gor was very real, he couldn't help wonder why the Chosen One would set Vegas on this path of such great power.

"That all sounds very exciting," Jen remarked when Vegas had finished his tale, "but it doesn't explain why you have come to see me."

Vegas sat ten feet away in a cross-legged position mimicking Jen. As he sat down, Jen felt Vegas' essence push against him. Not so much that it felt like an attack, it was more like a dog sniffing a person or another dog. Jen wasn't sure what to make of it, but it put him in more of a defensive state of mind.

"I need your advice," Vegas said once he was in the seated position. "It's no secret having powers has always been a goal of mine—"

"More like an obsession."

"True enough. However, I never dreamed of power on this scale. I can feel it changing me, turning me into someone I've always hated."

"The Chosen One of Legend?"

"Yes. But there is more to it than that. With this power, came a wisdom about the universe and about the human experience."

"Wisdom in itself can be a powerful tool when properly crafted."

"True, but—how powerful is wisdom when it brings no profit?"

"Wisdom was never meant to bring profit, but understanding and balance. That is a fundamental truth that most who seek enlightenment overlook. Profit is measured in how it affects one's self and to obtain true enlightenment. Self must be taken out of the equation. I believe you once said something that applies, 'Nothing is more elusive than an obvious fact.'"

Vegas intertwined his fingers, leaving his thumb and pointer finger straight, then positioned them on his chin as Jen often saw him do when he was in deep thought.

After several seconds he spoke, "I feel—a connection to a far off source—something I've never been aware of before, yet feel as though it has always been with me."

Jen rubbed his chin. "I'm not sure how much help I can be to you there, Vegas. Power is a very tricky thing to control. No matter how vast or incredible, power often has a source somewhere. My energies come from Earth and every living thing on the planet. Whatever source of power burning the entrails of the creature connected you to is anyone's guess, but your mind can be much more dangerous if left unchecked."

"How do you manage? You're probably the most powerful being on Earth. Yet hardly anyone outside of my circle knows who you are, let alone the extent of your powers."

Jen looked from Vegas' gaze and remembered everything that his "powers" put him through as a child. How he was bred to be the Human Weapon from an early age, and how the responsibility of his power had nearly driven him insane. Jen had gained much, but it was the losses which were forever with him that were impossible to forgive.

"The most important thing I can say to you, Vegas, is that you must do whatever you can to maintain your humanity. It is very easy to grow complacent and regard those without abilities, people that pose no threat to you, as expendable. Power, like money, doesn't bring happiness. No man or god is an island unto himself. We need companionship, love, to be truly at peace."

"But how, Jen? How can I control a force so awesome? How can I resist that which I can have, if I but will it? Observe." Vegas extended his hand then an orb of energy the size of a basketball appeared in his hand. The energy had a nucleus and spiraling parts that spun around the crimson ball of death. "This is all the energy it would take to wipe Las Vegas off the map forever. I could drop this and turn the entire city into nothing more than a giant sheet of glass in the desert. If I wanted to, I could kill everyone in the city. What is to stop me?"

"I see," Jen said remaining expressionless. "The biggest difference between men and gods, Vegas, is the freedom to choose what we want to be. Gods just—are. They have no real decisions about their character and often no way to change. Power does not corrupt as some would have you believe, but rather, it reveals. Similar to how alcohol releases a person's inhabitations, so to does the lure and acquisition of power. No matter how vast, the true measures of power comes from the man who wields it." Jen breathed in deeply and as he exhaled slowly, he waved his hand in front of the orb of destruction Vegas had created turning it instead into a golden ball of healing energy. If Vegas were to use it now, he would cure every person in every hospital in all of Las Vegas, as well as extend its inhabitants' lives by ten years. "A man is measured by the legacy he leaves. Now that you have this power will your legacy be one of death—or life?"

Vegas inspected the energy ball in his hands figuring out what Jen had made it able to do. "Why haven't you used this power before? If you can heal so many on such a scale, why not do so?"

"Because just as dangerous as power can be—so too is a man's ego. For every action there is a reaction, and history tells us that when something happens people often do not fully understand, chaos is born. Healing in that way would start a ripple that no one could contain. Anytime you use power to affect so many, you must always ask yourself—are you prepared for what comes next?" Jen waved his hand again this time forcing the energy orb in Vegas' hand to disappear.

A smirk etched Vegas' lips. "Thank you, Jen. I believe I know what I must do. Our time together was—eye opening. By the way, were you aware of why your parents chose to spell your name Jen instead of the traditional Jin?

"It has to do with Confucius and an ancient Chinese saying. 'Jen' was said to stand for a person's humanity, goodness, benevolence. Do you think your parents knew you would turn out the way you have when they chose to name you?"

Before Jen could reply, Vegas had disappeared in a flash of light leaving Jen alone again with his candles. Sweat began to bead at Jen's temple as worry set in. Vegas seemed pleasant enough, but he definitely wasn't himself. Jen had never told anyone why his name was spelled the way it was, most people never asked. The fact that Vegas knew now had several implications—none of which were positive.

Also no matter how hard he tried to shake the feeling—Jen couldn't help thinking the main reason for Vegas' visit was so he could compare his new power to Jen's. Coupled with the fact that Vegas and the others had left only an hour and a half ago, the shady smile and the abruptness with which Vegas left didn't fill Jen with much confidence in the future of the universe.

* * * *

Vegas was flying head first into Jupiter after his brief chat with Jen. Vegas knew he shouldn't, but he couldn't resist the urge to jump into the time stream as the Chosen One had done when he drafted Vegas for this mission. Vegas wondered what Jen was thinking. He tried to find out, but Jen had wisely kept up his mental defenses.

Pushing his mind from personal interest, Vegas focused on the mission at hand as he descended into Jupiter's atmosphere. So he wouldn't have to bother struggling against the winds that raged at an unprecedented nine hundred miles an hour, Vegas made himself intangible. The closer he got to the center of the planet, the more Typhon's power raged. Finally Vegas found Typhon, and created an invisible force field around himself while he let his body become tangible again. Vegas stood on air with perfect posture, relaxed with hands intertwined behind his back, waiting for Typhon to notice him.

When Typhon sensed he was not alone, he slowly turned to face Vegas. Typhon was the most bazaar creature Vegas had ever seen by far. The legends had always said Typhon was big, but he appeared more massive than Vegas expected. The Titan-god's size was so that it was like Vegas was about to do battle with a living being as big as the

Earth! He appeared man-shaped down to the thighs, with two coiled vipers in place of legs, which constantly slithered back and forth in the air. Attached to his hands in place of fingers were a hundred serpent heads, fifty per hand. He had enormous wings like an eagle; his face bore dirty matted hair and a beard, pointed ears, and eyes that flashed with fire. The strangest thing was that Typhon's head seemed to randomly shift between forms. Besides the head of a man, Vegas saw heads of bulls, boars, serpents, lions and leopards all morph onto Typhon, as if nature couldn't decide what horrible beast it wanted him to resemble, so it just threw them all together. With all that chaos, the only thought Vegas could muster was, *how and why is he so big?*

For a brief moment, it appeared Typhon was studying Vegas just as much as Vegas was studying him. Vegas could only wonder what Typhon was thinking, being confronted with a power that had never been released before. Typhon had no way of knowing what to expect. All he had was the false bravado of a Titan-god that had spent too much time at the top of the food chain and couldn't understand his time was up.

Typhon bellowed a hardy laugh of confidence. As he spoke, the planet reacted with flashes of lightning and the roar of raging storms. "You appear much smaller than I would have expected, mortal. Do you presume yourself my equal? The power of the Ophiotaurus was part of a prophecy to destroy the Olympian gods and Zeus, the usurper of Kronus' throne. Bow and call me master and I will—"

Before Typhon finished his sentence, Vegas used a burst of speed to close the distance between himself and Typhon. Then with a fist full of scarlet energy, he punched the great beast as hard as he could, sending it flying further into the murky haze of Jupiter. As Typhon fell deep into Jupiter, he shrieked and wailed with the cries of all the animals that appeared in his head. Vegas was annoyed with the pompous posturing and sheer audacity. It was obvious Typhon was trying to convince himself more than Vegas.

Vegas couldn't hold back a chortle as he thought about what Jen had said, "Gods don't get to choose what they are." Typhon had never faced someone potentially more powerful than him, but Vegas had made a lifetime of taking down enemies he shouldn't even be in the same zip code with. Remembering his past adventures brought on an emotion that Vegas couldn't describe, but somehow he felt that through the power he gained—he had also somehow—lost something. But what was it?

Before Vegas could ponder his feelings more, Typhon reappeared, his wings flapping mightily as they carried him into battle. His eyes burned with fury, his serpent fingers tightened, each primed and ready, yearning for blood and vengeance.

"You—dare!" Vegas heard rumble from every direction. Suddenly a wall of air slammed Vegas in the back sending him towards Typhon. Then the Titan-god flicked Vegas like an ant, making it his turn to go flying uncontrollably through the multi-colored haze. Vegas recovered quickly only to find Typhon closing in on him, bellowing his horrible battle cry, wings flapping, propelling him like an angel of death and destruction.

Vegas prepared himself for the attack, but before Typhon reached him, Vegas felt an intense charge of energy spark all around him. Before he could react, a lightning bolt bigger than some continents on Earth encompassed Vegas in its fury. Vegas looked at his arms and could see the red energies fade a little; he felt his connection to this power being tested. Yet, before he could give it any more credence, Typhon was on him again. Typhon began to hammer Vegas with thick clouds of wind and powerful lightning.

Typhon had gained the all-important momentum of battle and didn't show any signs of letting up. Along with the winds and lightning, Typhon also shot thick bursts of blue flames from his eyes that would've set fire to Earth's ozone. It was as if Vegas wasn't fighting Typhon as much as the Jovian giant Jupiter itself. With all of his new power, Vegas couldn't battle the both of them on the terms that Typhon had set.

Vegas kept taking the punishment inflicted on him by Typhon. He felt a growing sensation more like fatigue than pain. It was like his powers where short-circuiting revealing chinks in his armor. Vegas dug deep within himself finding emotions that had been locked away since he received the power. He let the power and emotions bubble until they reached just below the surface. Vegas gained control not letting the wind knock him around any longer. Then as Typhon closed in, both arms outstretched, the vipers that extended from each hand hissed spitting out acid. Typhon's eyes smoldered, his mouth open wide enough to swallow whole moons, his will forced unimaginably powerful lightning to twist towards his enemy.

"Enough!" Vegas screamed extending his arms releasing the energy that he had allowed to build. The energy came out in a sphere that extended from Vegas' body erupting and shining like a red star. Typhon was forced back and the maelstrom he had created on Jupiter blinked in its intensity.

Feeling his chance, Vegas flew upward at top speed. As he ascended, Vegas willed a ball of energy around Typhon and kept it connected to a line of energy that ran from his hand, so he could tow the Titan-god along behind him. When he broke the Jovian atmosphere, Vegas pushed his muscles to the limit pulling then flinging Typhon over his shoulder, finally releasing the figurative ball and chain.

Typhon twisted several times before he used his wings to stop himself. Of course, there is no wind for his wings to work in space, proving yet again that the laws of physics didn't apply to creatures like Typhon. When he stopped, Typhon had the sun behind him, his wings extended like an evil yet majestic eagle. His humanoid shoulders broad and powerful, his snake legs still slithering side to side and back and forth and his eyes gleaming as bright as the sun behind him. The Titan-god's silhouette looked like the most horrifying, terrible creature a person could dream up, like a nightmare of the most insane mind of ancient times made real.

Vegas saw from the corner of his eye that the gases, winds and lightning of Jupiter were slowly pulling away from the planet reaching like cold stiff fingers for Typhon. It was almost as though the entire planet was moving out of its orbit only to feel Typhon locked in its embrace once again.

With the last clue provided by the light of the sun shining behind Typhon, Vegas was able to see how he could put Typhon down easily and quickly—maybe even permanently. Typhon's eyes flashed and a burst of blue flames shot at Vegas as well as lightning bolts from Jupiter. Vegas slapped his hands together, more out of habit than necessity, which created a powerful explosion. The force of Vegas' hands coming together diverted both the fire and lightning sending them into the depths of space.

Vegas summoned the same dark red energy he had shown Jen that could lay waste to Las Vegas, increased its power tenfold, and then tossed it at Typhon. Typhon swatted it away, but when he did he left himself open for the tidal wave of force that came from Vegas' other fist. Typhon pushed back on Vegas' blast, but couldn't advance. Vegas took his free hand, pointed it toward Jupiter then extended energy to surround the planet, sequestering it from Typhon.

"Nooo!" Typhon thundered in the emptiness of space. Vegas felt Typhon wildly swing trying to swat the power that hit him like some cosmic waterfall, but it was too late. Vegas had completely cut Jupiter off and Typhon's size instantly reduced drastically. Although he was almost bigger than the Earth just moments before, he now appeared smaller than the Empire State building.

Becoming so small in stature, Typhon was no longer able to fight off Vegas' cosmic sprays, so he was hurled deep into space towards the sun at his back. Vegas flew after the Titan-god. When he caught up to it, he delivered a crippling blow to its humanoid stomach launching it even faster through the dark void. Again, Vegas gave chase, but this time he grabbed Typhon's ever moving snake-like lower half and towed the monster behind him.

At first Vegas was going to throw Typhon into the sun, but he thought that might kill him. What Vegas now understood about immortal beings was that while they can be vanquished, they can never be killed. Vanquishing Typhon would just plunge him into a realm of darkness from which he would eventually free himself and be reborn to terrorize Earth again. Instead, Vegas opened a portal and flew Typhon and himself through it finally emerging from the other end in front of the planet Mars.

Vegas let go of Typhon, but reinstituted the ball of energy around him and gripped the energy trail that connected it. Vegas tightened the ball of energy, making it as small as he could without crushing or killing Typhon, then closed his eyes and concentrated. He had no way of knowing if he could really pull off what he had planned—only a confidence in himself and a will to make his desires reality.

Vegas opened his eyes and saw straight into the eyes of Typhon. He was inside the tight ball looking very uncomfortable and very angry. Typhon muttered something, but Vegas paid no attention as his will was carried out. Typhon disappeared from sight along with the fizzling scarlet energy Vegas had created.

Smiling at the red energies that he bended to his will and with his warm-up was over, Vegas teleported again, this time to ready himself for the main event.

* * * *

With a whoosh of wind and a flash of light, Vegas popped back into the ship with Joe, Rob and Deep. They all jumped simultaneously, shocked at his arrival.

"What the fuck did you do out there? How did you beat that thing?" Joe demanded to know.

"Calm down," Vegas chuckled. "What were you guys able to see?"

"We saw da whole damn thang until Typhon shrunk like a frosted dick'n you blasted him into the great beyond!" Rob interjected.

"It was pretty simple really. Typhon was the Titan-god of the storm, so naturally his powers didn't work in space. When I separated him from Jupiter, the planet's atmosphere tried to reunite with Typhon and I noticed him shrinking, thanks to the sun beaming behind him. So I blasted him to Mars because it doesn't have an atmosphere and buried him under Olympus Mons."

"Interesting," Deep said rubbing his head. "If his powers can be so easily negated without an atmosphere, why wouldn't the Greek gods imprison him on a dead world like Mars in the first place?"

"Ah, the Greeks were always doing stuff like that. Making someone roll a rock uphill for all time, making Atlas hold up the sky, having birds eat someone's guts, healing him to let the birds eat all over again. They always laid out weird punishments. They like for the person ta be right on the edge of escape, but have no chance. Lock'n Typhon's power away on a planet dat he would be all powerful seems like some'n they would do," Rob answered.

"All right then," Joe said, clapping his hands one good time to get everyone's attention. "Now that you have that taken care of, could you please go save the universe and lock Gor away forever—pretty pleassssee?"

"Of course. You guys use the spacefold engines to get back to Earth. I have one more stop to make, then I'll deal with Gor."

"Oh, what the fuck, Vegas?" Joe barked in protest.

"Calm down, Joe, I know what I'm doing—trust me."

"It would make us all feel a bit better if you handled Gor first, Vegas," Deep said meekly.

Vegas paused to look at his friends. They all seemed to have come to a silent understanding and each had risked so much to come on this journey. They had done above and beyond everything he had asked, the least Vegas could do was give into their request—for now.

"Very well. My detour can wait a moment longer. Head back to Earth. I'll meet you there when this is finally over." With that, Vegas disappeared in a gush of wind and flash of light.

"Think he'll head straight to Gor?" Joe asked.

"Hard to say," Deep responded. "He seems very different. Besides the glowing skin and powers, his personality, his speech, inflection, it's all different as if the power has given him a new personality. I have—mixed feelings to say the least. I'm not sure how to describe it."

"Whelp, I feel like I just watched my mother-in-law drive off a cliff in my new BMW, if'n ya catch my drift," Rob surmised.

Deep rubbed his chin. "For some reason that analogy does make sense."

"I got it." Joe shrugged.

"You're the pilot, Joe. What's next?"

"You heard the Captain. Our mission in space is done, time to head home and pray for all this to finally be over."

* * * *

When the sensation of teleporting had gone, Vegas was floating about fifty miles from the event horizon of the super massive black hole in the center of the Milky Way. Vegas was highly enlightened, much wiser with a deeper understanding of the universe and its workings. Yet even with his vast power, he didn't care to charge into the event horizon of the black hole. Everything he had learned in physics had told him that the event horizon of any black hole, let alone a super massive one, was the point of no return. Not even light could escape once it crossed that line. Stars were shining brightly all around the black hole, as they orbited it like planets would a sun. Even though it was fifteen million miles across, from this distance the black hole looked like a massive perfectly black orb that had light dancing around it. Stars moved and shifted toward the black hole, some staying still as their energy was pulled off and sucked into nothingness. Two jets of gamma rays beamed forces violently from each end of the black holes as it sucked in too much energy too fast to contain it: all of this happened in the eerie silence of space.

Suddenly, it seemed as though Vegas' task was much more daunting than he realized. Even now Vegas wasn't sure he could survive the black hole. He wasn't sure how Gor could possibly be so powerful that he was feeding off of the power drawn in by something so massive as the quasar coming from the center. Plenty of things went through Vegas' mind, but fear wasn't one of them. He was cautious, but unafraid—which bothered him for some reason.

Pushing his thoughts aside, Vegas did the only thing he could do and called out to Gor's essence in the quasar. Vegas could feel Gor, not only near the center of the black hole, but all around him. Gor had placed most of himself along the event horizon; only a small piece of himself was near, but not actually in the center as Vegas had thought. The parts of Gor on the edges of the center absorbed the burped up gamma rays the black hole shot out, as well as some of the surrounding stars' energy, then disbursed the energy to the rest of his essence along the event horizon.

The situation wasn't as intimating as it first seemed. Even Gor didn't risk exposing so much of himself to the black hole, but still it was impressive that he could manage such feats as sparking a quasar in the first place. Now all Vegas had to do was find a way to either shatter Gor's essence so he couldn't form cognitive thoughts, or use any power at his disposal—but how was he going to do that? Vegas was working out options in his head, when an unexpected guest showed up with all the answers.

As Vegas floated staring into the heart of the quasar, The Chosen One of Legend paid him a visit, his astral-projected form appearing directly in front of Vegas.

"Vegas!" The Chosen One began smiling, his arms raised in victory. "You acquired the hidden power of the Titans. I knew you would succeed where all others would fail. I'm a little surprised you're naked, but good job."

"What are you doing here?" Vegas demanded. "I thought you were half dead somewhere."

"I am challenged yes—half dead, never." Chosen One chortled.

"Perfect. Then why don't you pop on over here and take care of your archenemy then, so I can go home. I wasn't sure how to do what needed done anyway."

"Afraid that isn't possible. Like I said I am being challenged, of course, I'm winning now, but I'm unable to break away."

"Why do I get the feeling you're lying to me?"

"Feel however you want. My answer isn't going to change. You've finished the hard part. To end this, you simply need to drain away Gor's energy and force his essence to opposite ends of the galaxy. This was a Hail Mary move for him, not easily duplicated."

"Wait, you mean that's it? After everything I've been though, no epic battle at the end. Just use my power to force my will—spread my hands and it's all over."

"Basically, yes. You sound disappointed."

"Of course, I'm disappointed! I thought I was doing this for something, for a big payoff. This is just so—anti-climatic."

"Vegas, fighting with the level of power you now possess, is much different than the battles you've had in the past. There is much less physicality when dealing with the powers of the cosmos. You'll rarely need to punch anyone or anything again."

"What? I've seen you throw punches and fight plenty of times."

"True, but I'm also forced to hold back most of the time. I'm from another dimension and most of my power is trapped in that dimension. I can access it, but not without consequences. Plus I often enjoy the challenge the handicap provides."

Vegas hung his head. That feeling of loss crept up on him again as if he had forsaken a part of himself, but he never realized until he lost it.

"Humm, for someone glowing red you look awfully blue. Cheer up, Vegas, this is what you always wanted, isn't it—to be my equal? You have your heart's secret desire You're now probably the second most powerful being in your universe."

Vegas looked up in time to see the same cocky smirk slide across Chosen One's lips letting Vegas know who Chosen One regarded as the first most powerful. Even with all Vegas had accomplished and proved, this bastard was still smug.

Deciding again to ignore his feeling Vegas asked, "Why couldn't you do this? If it's so simple and with so much time, you could've done this on your own."

Chosen One chuckled. "You give me too much credit. I could've attempted it, yes, but I believe forcing your will on Gor will be dangerous and stressful on your body and new found powers."

Something kept nagging at Vegas and wouldn't let him go. It was like having the last piece of a puzzle, but for some reason not being able to put it in place to complete the picture. Again, Vegas forced it aside.

"I can see you're deep in thought, so I'll leave you to your work. Don't underestimate Gor, even though you're going up against less than one tenth of his might, he is not to be taken lightly. Once you've finished, I expect you to join me on my quest across the cosmos."

"Wait—what? Why would I join you?"

"What else are you going to do? Return to Earth? Now there is nothing for you there. No challenge to test yourself any longer. Actually, I doubt anything in that galaxy could oppose you now. This is not Gor's only means of resurrection, there are pieces of him spread all throughout the universe. This is just the most recent and the most likely to succeed plan he has recently implemented. What better purpose would your powers serve, than to accompany me on my mission to stomp Gor from existence."

Again Vegas hung his head thinking about what Chosen One was saying and as much as he hated it—it made sense. Vegas could feel, that besides Gor, there were no challenges for him. Even Typhon was relatively easily beaten compared to the battles Vegas had won in the past.

"See you soon," Chosen One said, the arrogance lacing his voice, stinging like a cut from a poisoned-tipped sword. When Vegas looked up, Chosen One was gone having taken Vegas' self-assurance with him.

* * * *

Vegas wouldn't lie if you asked him—he did have plans for this power after he dealt with Gor, but traveling the cosmos with Chosen One definitely wasn't on his list. If there was anything Vegas hated, it was being put into a corner and not having the chance to choose his path. It was clear that something would have to be done to put things back in Vegas' favor, but for now he focused on the task at hand.

Closing his eyes, Vegas extended his senses out farther and farther until he finally found Gor huddled in the darkest corners of the event horizon, like a scared child sucking a bottle.

"You dare approach the omega! Do you presume that you cannot die by my hand mortal?" A deep, ominous voice growled in Vegas' head. The voice, drenched in evil and power, threatened to drown Vegas in hopelessness, despair, and self-loathing. The voice was unlike anything Vegas had heard even while in the temple of the Titans. The power in Gor's voice alone was truly awesome.

With as much confidence as he could muster Vegas began, "As a mortal I have slain dragons and other terrible creatures of Greek myths, I have beaten the defenses of the Titans and seized control of their fabled power, with that power I have defeated the great and powerful Typhon. I do not dare—I command you into nothingness."

The horrible voice cackled wildly in amusement before saying, "Your power is nothing compared to me even as I am now! Typhon is nothing more than a condom I would use to fuck your home world!"

Even with his mind so enlightened, Vegas thought that was some messed up shit to say. Vegas had encountered Gor once before when he almost resurrected himself thanks to a jewel that harnessed his power. He had inhabited a man and used him to try to pull the rest of himself together. He would've done it, too, if not for Chosen One showing up when he did. However, that meeting with Gor revealed a lot, like how he has to draw on the personality of his host in the first stages of symbiosis. As much as he didn't want to admit it that was something Vegas would've said to punk out an opponent. Gor was trying to use Vegas as an avatar to be reborn. Now that he was looking for it, Vegas could feel Gor pulling on his consciousness, trying to slowly strangle his soul, and then swallow it whole like an anaconda would its prey.

Still floating in space, Vegas crossed his legs keeping his eyes closed. With every ounce of concentration he had, Vegas tried to force Gor out and shatter him across the galaxy. However, Gor's constant ramblings didn't make his concentration very easy.

"You coward! You strike against me in my weakened state; if resurrected I could crush you with the power held in my mere finger."

Vegas concentrated doing his best to ignore the taunts. Slowly he felt himself tap into the vast power of the cosmos.

"Why do you oppose me? We have a common enemy and I care not for your planet Earth. It is a mere dot in my grand plans. Allow me to be reborn and I swear that your planet will be spared and he whom you hate will be crushed under my heel!"

Now, that actually sounded tempting. Yet, Vegas stayed focused on his goal. He felt his skin begin to fizzle and crackle. Power was pulsing outward from him as his will was enforced.

"Is this who you are? A coward who hides behind a vile of power, no contest of skill, no creativity, no use of your mind? Have you become so drunk with power that you are now an inane simpleton?"

Gor had struck a nerve with that last comment. Nothing had meant more to Vegas than his rational mind. It had accomplished feats others couldn't dream: Vegas had solved mysteries in physics others were decades away from discovering. Gor's taunts have shown Vegas how the last piece of the puzzle fit into the grander picture. Thanks to Gor, Vegas now understood how he felt and why, but more importantly what he was going to do about it.

Vegas' resolve stiffened. He had enough of Gor and was ready to be rid of him. First, Vegas reached out into the quasar and reversed the conditions Gor had set and changed it back into a regular super massive black hole.

"You will not be rid of me! Your universe will not be rid of me! I am immortal, I cannot die, and I cannot truly be defeated. You merely delay your death, but you can do nothing to stop your species extinction!"

The power in Gor's voice rose. Even though he couldn't reform himself, Gor was attacking, yet the attack didn't seem to be directed at Vegas. As quickly as he could, Vegas reached out and gathered every trace of Gor that had been accruing energy from the quasar giving it a solid form then forced it closer and closer to the event horizon.

What better way to defeat Gor, than with the very instrument he tried to use for victory. Vegas felt his body humming, buzzing wildly as power rained out of him. Off in the distance, Vegas detected a burst of power followed by some shift in space-time as if some sort of gateway had been opened. Whatever it was, Vegas could feel it was important and that it was Gor's doing. Gor was pushing against Vegas so he couldn't spare the time to investigate. If Vegas lost one trace of Gor, he could possibly ignite a repeat performance of today.

"Where will you go from here, mortal? Where will you go from here?" Gor snickered in the face of defeat.

At last, Vegas had forced Gor into the nothingness of the black hole and forced him behind the point of return. Vegas' power was slipping out in the directions of the event horizon; he could feel red crackles of power being ripped from his chest pulling him slowly into the black hole. Vegas had gotten too close as he forced Gor into the black hole. Some of his power was getting sucked in, and now Vegas attached to it, was also getting pulled closer to the point of no return. Feeling panic set in, Vegas clapped his hands together creating a massive explosion. The noiseless blast was enough to blow Vegas far enough back that he could move freely again.

The threat of Gor now vanquished, Vegas slightly relaxed, but when he did he noticed a change in himself. Accessing cosmic power on such a great scale had changed Vegas, his mind and heart seemed detached. The things that used to matter suddenly didn't, as if the use of power was an epiphany to his already enlightened mind. Before Vegas could soak in his newfound understanding, he turned and saw what Gor had done. With the power he had absorbed, Gor had somehow set off a hyper nova and opened a portal that ripped a hole into space-time. The hyper nova created a massive gamma ray burst that traveled through the portal. Vegas reached out with his enhanced awareness of all things cosmic, until he found when and where the rip in time opened. When he found its origin, a chill itched down Vegas' spine—the gamma ray burst was heading straight to Earth.

Chapter 18

As soon as he realized what Gor had done, Vegas called on the power cosmic with the full force of his will. Vegas extended his will outward until the very fabric of space-time was practically tangible. Vegas wrapped himself in his power until he existed outside of space-time. When he looked around, everything was frozen in place. The natural color of everything was distorted like he was looking at all there was through some type of circus mirror.

Gor was gone, the super massive black hole was back to normal, and Vegas had limitless power, but somehow he had still lost and Earth was still about to be destroyed. The portal Gor had opened was almost closed when Vegas froze time. The gamma rays had already burst well through the other end.

Everything had been like a deadly game of cards ever since Chosen One first came to Vegas telling him of the hidden power on Jupiter. Vegas thought he knew all the players at the table and most importantly all the hands that could be played. Gor had surprised Vegas with a trump card that let him wipe out not just Earth, but every planet in the solar system as easily as brushing dirt off his shoulders.

Vegas hovered in the cross-legged position, his hands resting in his lap, fingers gently touching each other like he had seen Jen do countless times. Vegas closed his eyes and concentrated. He used his power and knowledge of the universe to again invoke his will. Understanding that three dimisional space is one representation of reality, and the other exists on a flat two dimisional holographic film at the edge of the cosmos, Vegas reached out to that flat film of space-time at the edges of the universe. Taking the flat film of information in which all form in the universe is stored, Vegas bent and twisted it until he had wrapped himself in the fabric of space-time of what he now understood to be a finite universe.

Now existing outside the laws of time, Vegas relived the events that got him to this moment. He thought about Earth, about Chosen One, and most of all, he thought about what he wanted. The more he stayed outside time, the more the power cosmic rained into and then out of him. Vegas felt like a conduit for universal energies that he never knew existed and couldn't hope to fathom before his transformation. The more the energy flowed, the more it shaped who Vegas was and what he wanted. Vegas tested Gor's work and found the fail-safes and insurances that he put in place. Vegas had to admit he admired Gor's thoroughness.

Much time passed—yet none at all, when Vegas decided on a course of action out of the conditions Gor left. If it was something he would've done before he became all powerful—Vegas wasn't sure. The only thing he could say with certainty was that it was the most rational thing for him to do.

* * * *

Fuck, Vegas! Topaz thought to herself for the twelfth time since leaving Vegas' place. She still couldn't believe she had even gone at all, let alone stayed long enough for him to spout off his bullshit. Jen trying to calm her down had only pissed her off even more. The fact that the man that had mentored her for months in the use of her powers and in tranquility and balance was taking up for that—bastard, Vegas! Jen had talked like she was overreacting. Vegas says we have to drop everything, to do what he commands and leave now to save the universe. How do you under react to that?

Tired, frustrated and annoyed beyond belief, Topaz threw her clothes off as soon as she was in her apartment then headed for the shower. The shower had been so relaxing, she almost forgot about Vegas and his lies, his arrogance, his gorgeous smile and beautiful golden chestnut eyes. No one got on Topaz's nerves more than Vegas and the fact that he was so damn good looking just pissed her off. It wasn't right that someone who was such an ass could look so good. Topaz let the water cascade over her, washing everything away. It washed away her anger, her doubt in if she should have gone with Vegas. All her confusion and anxiety was flowing down the drain hopefully never to be seen again.

She milked the shower until the hot water ran out and then she grabbed a towel, wrapped it around her hair, exiting the bathroom humming her favorite Erica Badu song. Topaz didn't make it two steps out of her bathroom when she saw a brilliant crimson fluorescence in her living room.

"Hello Topaz," the source of the red glow said calmly enough, but it still was enough of a surprise to Topaz that she screamed and fell to the ground. On instinct, she tapped into the power from the diamond earrings she never took off and threw up a barrier.

"Who are you?" Topaz demanded. She also took in every detail of the intruder's appearance and did her best not to let it affect her. Whoever this guy was; he had the body of a god. His skin was red with twinkles of starlight all over, yet his muscles were visibly carved like a statue. Plus the fact he was completely naked and hung like a horse didn't make it any easier for Topaz to focus. If having powers had taught her nothing else about the super hero world and life in general, she knew not to let a beautiful man with powers get her all hot and bothered. The better looking often means the more evil.

"I didn't mean to startle you. I wasn't aware of what you were doing at this point in time, only where you were. I apologize for my timing."

Topaz remembered that she was butt-naked, but was afraid to move to cover herself, not willing to give any slack to her shield. As much as she hated it the human Christmas light had her full attention.

"Imma ask one last time before I blast you on your ass, Rudolph. Who are you?" Topaz stipulated as she gingerly rose to her feet, still wet and naked but now dripping just as much with confidence as she was water. Energy increased around her fist and eyes as she drew on the power from her earrings and another piercing she preferred to keep private, but it was a little too late for that now.

"Relax, Topaz. It's me."

"Sorry, last time I checked I didn't know anybody that was a giant traffic light—except the Chosen One sometimes, and you definitely aren't him."

"Perhaps this will help." The intruder's eyes seemed to close then the glow around his skin began to fade slightly. His skin was still somewhat red, but it took on a more brown hue. His muscles kept their form and shape, but looked more normal—more human. Topaz stayed focused on the man's face, but noticed the horse cock didn't go anywhere.

Then Topaz was mortified when she recognized the face behind the light, "Vegas!"

"None other."

"….Bullshit…."

But as she looked closer into the face, thought about the voice, Topaz knew it was true. Topaz dropped her shields, but picked up her towel on the floor along with her anger.

Vegas—it was fucking Vegas! She was so mad she couldn't speak as she wrapped herself in her towel.

"Please allow me." Vegas extended his hand then a flash of light hit Topaz and she was completely dry and fully dressed. She was wearing her favorite pair of black yoga pants and her favorite yellow sports bra that she often worked out in. Her hair was dry and styled how she would've done it if she had time, plus her finger and toenails were done better than any stylist Topaz had ever went to. The light also imposed a feeling of confidence and sexiness stronger than Topaz usually felt on her own. Still—she was pissed and annoyed at Vegas all over again.

Before she could start in on him he spoke, "See, I told you I was telling the truth."

She was so livid and thinking so fast that her mouth couldn't form the words that were whizzing through her mind. Her hands were shaking and she was sure someone could read her pulse by looking at her forehead because of how hard her blood was pumping.

"I—I think I should start with the obvious," Vegas began. "If I've timed this right, you left my place about an hour ago, I haven't left for Jupiter yet. Only Rob, Deep and Joe decided to come with me and—"

"What are you and why are you naked?" Topaz demanded.

Vegas looked down as if he was unaware he had appeared in nothing but his shiny new birthday suit, "Oh, I forgot. I don't feel the need for clothes. I guess I was also hoping you would be impressed—are you?" Vegas smiled.

Topaz quickly scanned Vegas then rolled her eyes. "No, I'm not," she lied.

"I could place some clothes on if it makes you uncomfortable."

"It's whatever, Vegas, just tell me what you're doing here," Topaz said as nonchalantly as possible then pried her eyes off Vegas and walked into the kitchen. Topaz did her best to look as annoyed as possible.

"I can see your patience is wearing thin, so I'll get to the point of my visit."

"That would be best," Topaz said after taking a bottled water out of her refrigerator and slamming the door.

"I saved the universe, but I failed Earth," Vegas said expressionless.

"Come again."

"I was able to stop Gor. He will not be able to use Earth or even the Milky Way as a method of his resurrection again. His only hope is throughout the vast darkest corners of the cosmos."

Topaz began to eat an apple not so much because she was hungry, but to give her something to look at besides Vegas. "Great—good job on that. So how did you fail the Earth and what are you going to do about it? More importantly what does it have to do with me?"

"I had defeated Gor. I was about to banish him from the Milky Way, when he played a trump card I didn't see coming. He took one of the biggest stars in the Milky Way then forced it into a hypernova. The explosion created a massive amount of energy and destructive force called a gamma ray burst. Then, Gor also opened a tear in space-time that went back six thousand years while pointing the portal towards our solar system. By moving the star, causing it to explode in the past, and aiming it at Earth, Gor was able to wipe out the entire solar system with a gamma ray burst in what you can say is my present."

Topaz wasn't sure if it was the fact that she had been forced to listen to Vegas so much in the past, or if it was the new way he delivered information, but she actually understood all that.

"Soooo, Gor moved a star into position, blew it up and timed it so that it will destroy everything in—"

"Ten hours from now."

"Right. And instead of trying to stop this—"

"Gamma ray burst."

"Right. Instead of trying to stop this gamma ray burst and saving everyone on the planet, you used your new powers to come back in time to see me?" Topaz surmised.

"That is accurate."

"You mother fucker," Topaz screamed. "You're trying to get your fuck'n dick sucked again aren't you! Let me guess, I suck you off and you'll have to strength to save everybody! You sick fuck!"

"On the contrary," Vegas said extending his hand again, power shining off his skin and his eyes morphing into orbs of scarlet energy. "Earth is doomed and I—I am above such things now. Allow me to show you."

Then before Topaz could protest, light flashed from Vegas' body. When Topaz's eyes adjusted, the strangest terrain she had ever seen surrounded her. The sky was purple with thick swirling clouds. There were rivers with a blue hue all around as well as multi-colored orange and red mountain ranges everywhere. The biggest shock came when she looked in the sky and didn't see the moon or the sun but three planets, one with rings like Saturn's. The other two were smaller, but just as beautiful as there natural color mixed with the purple atmosphere.

"I hope this world is visually pleasing to you," Vegas said appearing behind Topaz, again surprising her almost knocking her on her backside.

"Where the hell are we?"

"We're on a planet's moon that is on the opposite side of the Milky Way than Earth. You'll be safe from Gor's gamma ray burst here."

Topaz's heart beat increased as she began to understand what Vegas was doing. The cold reality hit her like some frosted wind off the lake of despair and isolation. The chill penetrated Topaz deeply, even making her teeth ache.

"You're going to let it happen, aren't you? You're going to let everyone die."

Vegas' face became as solemn as Topaz had ever seen him. His body language was lacking its usual swagger and confidence. He closed his eyes and the red light from his skin began to fade until he looked like his normal self again. Topaz recognized his smooth sienna brown complexion, his golden brown eyes, his freshly bald head and perfectly trimmed goatee. Topaz always hated that he looked so damn good when he was always so much of an ass. Even though he had changed his appearance back to normal, he apparently forgot that he was naked—Topaz didn't see a reason to say anything for the time being.

"That's the thing Topaz—it's already happened." There was a blandness in Vegas' voice that Topaz didn't understand. He looked the same as before, but his personality was just as foreign.

"What do you mean it's already happened? You came back in time, right? So go back in time again and save the world."

"I'm afraid it isn't that simple."

"And why not?"

"Gor was very ingenious about his execution. He somehow knew how to prevent me from traveling back in time far enough to stop him from launching his attack in any real meaningful way."

The more Vegas spoke, the more Topaz didn't recognize him. Vegas was being short winded and vague. She couldn't remember a time when Vegas didn't jump at the opportunity to run on about how brilliant he was, plus he had said Gor had done something ingenious, Vegas never said that about anyone but himself. Also, Vegas had always been a horn-ball, at least to Topaz. She couldn't remember a time when they were in the same room together and Vegas hadn't looked at her, at least once, like he wanted to jump her. Vegas had seen Topaz butt naked just moments before and now she was decked out in one of her favorite outfits feeling extremely attractive, yet he was still limp. That annoyed the hell out of Topaz, but she forced herself not to comment on it.

"What do you mean by that?" Topaz asked.

Vegas turned to Topaz expressionless, yet Topaz saw a weight and seriousness in his eyes.

"Come with me and I'll explain," Vegas said with a slight grin as he extended his hand to Topaz. She wasn't sure why but that tiny gesture was enough to shoot butterflies into her stomach. She slowly took Vegas' hand, cursed herself for feeling like some teenage girl and fought back a smile with all her might.

When she took Vegas' hand, they began to float high above the ground. As they stood still the mountains, valleys, lakes and streams, slowly moved below them. It was like an invisible escalator had carried them through the sky just below the multi-colored luster of the clouds.

Topaz observed the alien world's beauty for several seconds before Vegas began to speak. "There is more than one way to travel back in time. I will spare you all the semantics, but one way allows you to alter history and the other does not. Instead of changing something in the present, you will create an alternate reality. With the provisions Gor has put in place, I would only be able to create an alternate reality where our Earth survives. I have chosen not to do this."

Again not like Vegas. That was a very simple explanation of something very complex.

"Why? Why wouldn't you do it?"

"There are several moral implications that apply."

"Like?"

"Like the fact that it is the easiest option, but not the only?"

"Well, what's the other option?"

"It involves a lengthy explanation, but it basically would be very difficult for me to survive and my powers would likely be lost."

A twinge of anger began to boil in Topaz. Vegas was willing to let the entire human race go extinct just to save his own ass! But Vegas continued, before Topaz could voice her objection.

"I haven't made this decision lightly. But Gor is not fully defeated. As long as a trace of him survives, the entire universe is in peril. Life on Earth is all you know, but I can assure you that life on Earth is not all the life that exists in the cosmos. The logical thing, the only real rational thing to do, is to help Chosen One defeat Gor now that I have the ability to do so."

"And what about all our friends and family? You're just willing to let them die?"

"I don't have any family. I was raised on the streets for as long as I can remember. And I don't exactly have any friends."

"Rob, Deep, Blu, Zolomon, you don't consider any of them friends!"

"No more than they consider me one. They tolerate me out of necessity."

"Then what about me? Why did you come back to save me Vegas?"

Topaz felt Vegas' grip gently tighten around her hand. He turned to her and looked her straight in the eye and said the last thing Topaz thought she would ever hear Vegas say, "I love you."

"Excuse me?" Topaz managed as her heart jumped into her throat.

"I believe I always have. In my enlightened stated there is much I have learned about the universe and a lot I have learned about myself. I think I was a bit of a psychopath before."

"You needed cosmic enlightenment to tell you that?" Topaz joked, still flustered.

"Unfortunately, I'm serious. I didn't experience emotions like most people. Empathy, regret, happiness, love, I never really felt any of them before. I believe I am—incapable of such emotions. My rational and intelligent mind was the only thing I truly cared about. But there was always you. I was always drawn to you and never understood why—until now."

Topaz tried to pull away from Vegas so she could think straight. She fought the urge to hug him. The universe was at stake so this was no time to act girly. Deep down this is what Topaz wanted, but she also knew it wasn't right.

"I know what the right thing to do is," Vegas said. "I am willing to let everyone I've ever known die. I am willing to let the whole Earth be destroyed and even with my new awareness and emotions, I had no regrets about my decision—until I thought of never seeing you again. I wasn't willing to let you go."

It was the most romantic thing anyone had or ever would say to Topaz. She couldn't image ever feeling more wanted or more—special. But it wasn't right. If she let Vegas go through with this, how could she live with herself?

"This is just the beginning of what I can show you, Topaz. There are thousands of worlds throughout the galaxy that support life. You could be queen of anyone you choose. I could take you to worlds where you would be worshiped as a goddess, worlds where your slightest desire would be someone else's only goal in life. On different worlds your life would be prolonged. On some your powers would be magnified, your options are limitless. You have only but ask and I will deliver whatever you want."

A rush of temptation swept over Topaz. She had no family and Vegas had always been the most stable thing in her world, which said a lot about her life. All her problems gone, anything she wanted given to her in the blink of an eye—who wouldn't want that? But it just wasn't right. It wasn't in her nature to be so selfish.

"Do you really love me, Vegas?"

"I do."

"Will you really do whatever I ask?"

"I will."

Topaz took a deep breath. "Then I want you to fix this. I want you to stop the gamma ray burst."

"It is not logical for me to sacrifice myself for others that don't mean anything to me. Though enlightened, I am still human. I have no desire to die."

"Then don't die. The Vegas I knew wouldn't accept that he was beaten—he wouldn't accept that he had been outwitted and out-strategized. I understand why you don't care about the Earth. No one helped you growing up, no one gave you the credit you deserve, but you care about me, and I care about our home."

"It is irrational. The needs of the many far outweigh the wants of the few or the individual."

"What good is your power and knowledge if you're alone?"

"I could never truly be alone. I am one with the cosmos, one with the infinity of space. There is much more to the universe than you could ever hope to comprehend."

"Then you're ready to sacrifice our planet and everyone on it?"

"A sacrifice would suggest that there was something I was unwilling to lose. I do not consider this a sacrifice. Gor attempted to hurt me by destroying something he thought I cared about, but my time existing outside of time has changed my priorities."

"You're full of shit."

"Excuse me?"

"You're full of shit. Here you are floating, surrounded by more beautiful landscapes than anything I've ever imagined. You're talking funny like you had this great and profound realization about life and the universe, but yet you're still selfish."

"I'm willing to give up everything I want for the greater good of the universe. How is that selfish?"

"What are you giving up Vegas? You just said that you didn't care about Earth or anyone on it. You weren't willing to lose me—if you were, I wouldn't be here with you. I'm also starting to see even though you claim to love me, you brought me here out of your own selfishness. You never asked me what I wanted. If you truly care about someone, what matters to them has to matter to you. There may be much more out there, but I don't care. Earth is my universe, it is my everything, Vegas—Earth matters."

Vegas paused for several seconds as he looked out into the distance of the strange paradise he had brought them to. "If I do this and survive," Vegas began, "I will be the same as I always was. Incapable of being the man you want or the man you deserve."

"I know."

"And you're willing to let that go?"

"No, but I'm willing to sacrifice. If it's your love or everyone on Earth—then I have to pick Earth, Vegas. I have to."

"Very well, Topaz. You've made me realize that not everything in the universe is as predictable as I thought. I will try—for you."

Vegas reached and grabbed Topaz around the waist, pulled her close and then kissed her. Topaz felt the hardness of Vegas' body pressed close to hers. She felt his muscles like smooth granite, the thickness between his legs swell slightly against her as she melted in emotions she had long buried for Vegas scuttled to the surface. It was the best kiss she ever had in her life. She savored the moment because she knew she would likely never experience it again. Her hands grew warm as she felt Vegas' flesh morph into energy. A powerful glow radiated from everywhere at once and then without another word Topaz was back in her apartment—and Vegas was gone.

* * * *

Vegas wasn't very self-sacrificing before he had become enlightened, which made his current actions that much more perplexing. He was about to put his power and his life on the line for a species he no longer felt any connection to. None of them would know what he had done; none of them would so much as thank him. He had nothing to gain and everything to lose. His only motivation was the look of desperation in Topaz's eyes. In them, he saw what life was truly worth. He saw something worth protecting, worth fighting for, and even worth dying for.

With his vast power and intelligence, Vegas still found it difficult to navigate the time stream. Gor had somehow put barriers in the fabric of space-time that prevented him from traveling far enough back in the past to prevent the gamma ray burst. Every time Vegas tried to manipulate the fabric of space-time, he would be met with a force of energy. The harder he pushed against the force, the more pain he felt.

There was only one way Vegas could save Earth without creating a brand new reality. Vegas teleported where he was hovering just above the solar system, where the gamma ray burst would originate. He was going to have to open a portal large enough to absorb the whole maelstrom of gamma rays causing it to skip the solar system shooting out beneath it. Gor had locked up the time stream, so he couldn't move the burst back into the past or even into the distant future. Vegas was convinced Gor had set him up. It was either let the Earth be destroyed or Vegas' powers pushed to an extreme and possibly burn out his mortal body.

He could feel the gamma ray burst rushing forward at unbelievable speeds. It was like an invisible shadow of death, a tidal wave of demise and bereavement that would obliterate anything it came across. A gamma ray burst was so powerful it could put out more energy in seconds than a star would put out in its entire ten billion year lifetime. That was the kind of power he was up against.

Extending his left hand, Vegas reached out with his senses. He had to match the size of the portal Gor used to bring the gamma ray burst to the present. If it was too small, he wouldn't be able to contain the whole burst, too big and he would waste more energy than he needed causing him to not be able to maintain the portal long enough. Using the same process as the space fold engines he created, Vegas opened a wormhole.

Just as the wormhole opened, the gamma ray burst silently smashed into the portal with an onslaught that was actually pushing him down toward the solar system. Vegas extended both hands and held firm with all his might. His power pushed back on the burst of fatality willing the portal not to collapse from the intense pressure.

The gamma rays mixed with Vegas' crimson energies creating a blinding light brighter than any sun. The light dimmed Vegas' scarlet skin as well as everything else around him. It was as if he was in a room void of depth and form. He couldn't see his arms in front of him; it was the exact opposite of standing in a pitch black room. The strain on Vegas' body kept building. The pressure on his body was incredible. He doubted Atlas felt as much pain when he was forced to hold up the sky. Vegas opened his mouth in a soundless scream, pushing, holding the portal, his body burning from the inside out. The only thing he had to assist him was the love he felt for Topaz. He had placed her back in her apartment, so if Vegas failed, she died—and that was unacceptable. Never before had Vegas given so much of himself to something. He had never tried so hard at anything, never wanted anything as badly as he wanted Topaz to live.

Just as he thought he would be burned alive by his own power, the light faded and the pressure wasn't far behind. He was drained, more tired than he had ever been. This power was limitless, but his body wasn't. Vegas felt his eyes close as he fell into darkness. He didn't know if his plan had worked. He didn't know if the Earth was safe or if he would have the power to survive, but he let everything go. As his eyes closed, Vegas envisioned where he wanted to be, seeing it perfectly in his mind, then he surrendered to what he thought was the sweet embrace of death.

Chapter 19

Vegas thought he was dead. He thought there was no hope for him, that he would be lost to float the dark void of space forever, yet his eyes slowly crept open and the blurry frame of a woman came into focus.

"Topaz?" Vegas spoke weakly, "What—how—"

"I believe I can answer that!" Vegas heard Joe say from somewhere off to the side. Vegas' vision was still hazy, but he could see Joe standing over him grinning ear to ear. "You teleported back onto the ship after that light show."

"What light show?" Vegas muttered.

"You know what I'm talking about. We figured you had something to do with it. The whole sky was shining red. It was so bright people saw it during the day. People thought the world was ending man—it was some real spooky fury of God type shit. What were you doing up there?"

Vegas struggled to get up. "Rob, Deep—they—"

"They're all right," Joe answered as Topaz gently forced Vegas back down. "Rob went to visit his family, Professor Willis is back to his old self, but in some kind of funk for some reason. Other than that, everything's fine. Blu, Zolomon, and Jen stopped by. I think they all feel pretty shitty for not coming with us. A couple of people you called that didn't bother to show up when you told us about everything, stopped by too, like Panther, Tatum and Power Scorch, I definitely remember. Scorch has the right name man—that woman is hot as shit! Want that chick to sit on my face—oh, Panda Jack popped by, too. I think he was going to kill you, until I told him Rob and Deep were here—I have no idea what that was about."

Vegas' head felt like it was split open. His body was aching everywhere. He tried to move or speak, but it wasn't happening. Vegas caught Topaz giving Joe a nod.

"Whelp, I know when I'm sucking all the sexual tension out of a room. I'll be back to visit, Vegas. We'll be on our next adventure in no time." Joe said as he left.

"How do you feel?" Topaz asked.

"Like a deer that got hit by an eighteen wheeler on the highway."

"That's better than you look, so you should be fine."

"Haha."

Vegas looked at his surroundings. He was clearly in his lab in Las Vegas, but he had no idea how he had gotten there. The last thing he remembered was redirecting the gamma ray burst, and then trying to teleport back into the ship. He didn't think he had enough energy left to make it, but he must have. He was lying in a tub and his whole body was covered in a thick gray paste that smelled awful.

"It's your E.C.M powder," Topaz commented, seeing Vegas examining the paste, "Jen had some healing potion of his own he brought by. He said it should speed up your recovery even more. Don't ask me what's in it. I think Jen believes that the worse the concoction smells, the faster it works. He used it on me a couple of times. I'm curious though, why couldn't we just put those nannites back into your blood stream?"

"It's a very tricky process to introduce them. It would be very easy for them to kill me or take over my body and become sentient or something. I have to do it in a certain way."

"Well, you're still awake before any of us thought you would be. Except Joe, he started a bet on how long it would take you to wake up. We all owe the little bastard a hundred dollars."

"You didn't think I was going to wake up? Where's the faith?"

"He only beat me by one day."

"Tell me what I missed when I was out."

Vegas listened to Topaz as she described what had happened after he had blacked out. When he appeared on the ship, Vegas' body had second and first degree burns covering his entire body plus several broken bones. With Rob and Deep's help, Joe was able to follow a set of instructions Vegas had left if something happened to his body while using the avatar. Jupiter and its moon including Io had somehow returned to normal, but the astrological community was in an uproar trying to figure out what had happened. Several apocalyptic cults sprung up because of the gamma ray burst lights, and Topaz didn't tell anyone what Vegas had done—not that anyone would believe her any way. Over the last couple of nights, the planet had experienced beautiful auroras, again likely, due to the gamma radiation's effects on the sun. Other than that, nothing had changed. Earth was safe as it ever was.

"I still can't believe I'm alive," Vegas said, "Powerless yet again, but alive."

"I'll never forget what you did that day, Vegas. It was extremely brave of you."

Vegas chuckled. "Brave, huh. Don't know if I would call it that. Bet you wish you came along now right?"

"No."

"No?"

"I don't wish I would've gone with you to Jupiter. I was pissed off and I didn't believe you. It's not like you gave me much reason to trust you in the past."

Vegas' smirk returned. He struggled but managed to hold Topaz's hand in his, "And what about now?"

"Now—we take things slow," Topaz said pulling her hand away from Vegas.

"Why do you want to take it slow? I know you care about me."

"True, and you care about me, but you're still you, Vegas. I was pissed at you for a reason—a damn good one at that."

"That was then. I've changed."

"Changed what, Vegas? What have you changed, really?"

Looking up into Topaz's eyes, Vegas saw desperation similar to what he saw on that world he brought them to on the other side of the galaxy. She wanted to believe him; she wanted things to be different. Vegas could tell she was waiting for him to say something reassuring, something that would let her know that some type of feelings existed within him. He wanted to tell her there was something, but the more he searched inside himself the less he found. He cared for her, but it wasn't the same.

"That's what I thought. I'll be back to check on you soon and bring you some food. You have to be getting hungry," Topaz said then she got up to leave the room.

"I don't want to lose you."

Topaz stopped in the doorway and looked over her shoulder at Vegas. She had never looked more beautiful and strong. As she spoke, her words were firm and resolute, "You aren't losing me Vegas, but I'm afraid you can never really have me either."

As she turned to leave, Vegas could see a tear cascade down her cheek. Vegas couldn't remember a time Topaz looked so vulnerable, so exposed. She really cared—she maybe even loved Vegas now.

When Vegas was alone, he let his body relax and a gratifying smile carved its way along his lips. He had done the impossible; he had become a god and done what no other human being could hope to do—and he had lived. Vegas felt very pleased with himself. He knew challenges on this scale would be few and far between, but he had savored every last second. Vegas closed his eyes and let himself release all the tension and anxiety he had felt since the Chosen One of Legend showed up in his office sending him on this quest.

As Vegas let himself heal, all he could think of was what the universe would do to test him next and what new challenges would come along to let him prove he was the shit over and over again.

Epilogue

It had taken two days covered in the E.C.M paste for Vegas' body to fully recover and another week for to him to successfully reintroduce the nannites into his blood stream. Vegas retreated into the seclusion of his lab and the comforts of his mind, exercising both his body and brain every day. He thought about letting the world know what he had done, but Vegas realized even with their education of his deeds, there was no reciprocity to be had. The right people would know and that was all that mattered. After three weeks of intense training, boredom set in and he finally felt he was ready to start working again.

He sat in his office and looked through the different assignments that had poured in during his sabbatical. Some looked interesting. Vegas realized he had to lower his expectations. Opportunities to do things like go to Jupiter and fight Chimeras and dragons would definitely be few and far between. For now it was your usual drug bust, retrieval of stolen goods, killing people that deserved killing, and setting up people that didn't deserve being set up, the occasional super villain and government contracts. Rob, Deep, Jen or somebody he knew would get themselves in some kind of trouble soon like they always did and that was always interesting.

As Vegas ruffled through folders and videos of potential clients, a quick strike of light hit the center of his office. An invisible gust of energy knocked over his papers and other assortments throughout the office—The Chosen One of Legend had decided to pay Vegas another visit.

"I believe congratulations are in order," Chosen One said, hands behind his back nodding in respect.

"I wasn't expecting to see you at all now that I'm powerless."

"Of course, you did. You knew I would be by Vegas, but I admit I didn't want to stop by while you were—recovering. I only enjoy your company when you're at your best."

"Well as you can see, I'm fully recovered. Now if you could rearrange my office the way it was before you showed up and leave, I can consider this visit only slightly annoying. At least you showed up in person this time."

"Don't worry, I won't be staying long. But we have something to talk about and I believe I made a promise that I intend to keep."

Vegas sat back in his chair and reclined into the darkness of the office. His eyes never left Chosen One's, each of his fingers touched as he prepared to listen to what Chosen One had to say.

"Go on," Vegas insisted.

"First, I'm curious if you want to know what happed to the power you willingly relinquished."

"What are you talking about? I didn't 'relinquish' anything."

"Do not think you are anything but transparent to me, Vegas. Just because you found a way to lock me out of your mind now doesn't me I cannot read you. I know full well what you did, how you did it, and why."

I had forgotten how much I hate this bastard.

Vegas returned Chosen One's gaze even as his eyes hummed and fizzed with red energy. For Vegas it was like looking into dim suns, living power.

"You could've maintained your powers after shifting the gamma ray burst to the other side of the solar system. You could've joined me in hunting down Gor's remains throughout the universe, granted I do not need you to accomplish my task, but your help would've speeded up the process. Instead, you returned the power to Jupiter restoring the planet to its former state. Do you really hate me that much that you would throw away limitless power to avoid traveling the cosmos with me?"

Yes—yes I do.

"As usual you assume everything revolves around you," Vegas said deciding to be candid, if for no other reason than the truth would confuse and annoy Chosen One more than anything else. "I gave up the power for myself."

"Why?" Chosen One asked. It was obvious to Vegas Chosen One couldn't grasp why someone would give up the power of a god—why someone would want to be mortal.

"Because, you're a pussy."

"You dare!" Chosen One barked, his eyes poured out light and energy illuminating Vegas' entire office, yet Vegas didn't so much as flinch. "Do you forget to whom you speak? I am the most—"

"The most powerful being in the universe, I'm aware," Vegas said cutting off Chosen One, "but where is the challenge in that? What type of effort do you ever have to put into what you do? How often do you have to try at anything? What are you really without those powers of yours? How awesome would you be without them, huh? I've experienced the power cosmic and, I guarantee, I could've given Joe that power and he could've used it just as well as anyone else.

"It's a cheat. As I am, I've went up against monsters and villains so powerful I don't belong in the same state as them, let alone winning a fight against them. But I've beaten them all with nothing but my own intelligence and wit. When I had powers, there was no real sense of fear to drive me, no intense will to live. I thought power was what I wanted, I thought it was what I needed, but I now realized if anyone should be envious in this room—it should be you."

The power in Chosen One's eyes dispensed and the same cocky, arrogant smirk sliced across his lips.

"I wasn't aware of how ignorant you were until now, Vegas. Truly you are a fool."

"To each his own."

Chosen One chuckled. "Very well. I believe I owe you some answers."

Chosen One began explaining various secrets of the universe to Vegas. How gods existed in each of the billions of galaxies throughout the cosmos, each of the gods inhabiting the worlds of the galaxies, some weaker, some stronger, than the ones in the Milky Way. Throughout the galaxy's history they would take turns, turning on each other, killing one another as they faded in and out of mortal legends. Chosen One gave greater understanding into the principals Vegas had taken from his time as a cosmic being and exposed things Vegas hadn't considered.

Chosen One also explained the significance of Gor as a universal evil and how he was the opposing force of good that countered Gor. Chosen One also went on to say that due to Vegas' actions some of the Greek mythological beings of old might have returned to the world of the living. That was a problem Vegas wasn't ready to deal with and wouldn't deal with for the time being.

"I have fulfilled my end of our bargain," Chosen One said when he had finished. "I'll take my leave."

"Wait!" Vegas shouted before Chosen One could teleport. "There's one more thing."

"Yes," Chosen One hissed in irritation.

"When I was an all powerful ass whip, I felt a strange connection to an outside source. It was something different than the power of the cosmos and other universal energies. Have you ever felt anything like that before?

"No. Did you sever the connection before you gave up your power?"

"Yes."

"Do you feel any different?"

"I feel—freer."

"Interesting. I will look into it."

"Thanks. I believe you know the way out."

Chosen One turned to Vegas as he teleported out of the room. As he left, he created a much flashier display than his previous teleports. He made and held eye contact with Vegas until he left saying, "It will be interesting how your companions react to your acts of duplicity. Not everything is as you let them believe, especially Topaz. It will be an exciting time when she discovers your true feelings, don't you think?" Again Vegas caught that arrogant smile through the haze of energy. "Until next our paths meet, Vegas Baby."

And with that Chosen One was gone, and Vegas was left alone in his office. His papers and other items were still scattered throughout like a tornado was in the room seconds before.

Prick.

Acknowledgments

Well, was that fun or what? I had a really good time writing this novel and I can't believe it only took me about four months! The characters have been in my head for years and the story really did just kind of write itself. I've always been interested in science and astronomy and ancient myths from Greece and Egypt so it just felt right to combine them all into one pulse pounding adventure. I hope you enjoy what you read here, Vegas Baby will return in a all-different setting with brand new challenges. Vegas will be in every book but his cast will change through out the series, so I hope you like Vegas enough to put up with more of him. I just want to thank God first of all. I feel like there is a lot planned for me and these novels are the avenues that will take me where I need to be. Thanks to everyone who supported me, to everyone who helped edit (Tonya, Susan and Marrisa) if anything is wrong in this book it's my fault I'm sure. Thanks to everyone who will read this. Keep a look out because the next chapter in Vegas Baby's life will be ready before you know it, just have to finish the next book in my Divine Ability series first. If you're interested in murder mysteries check out my first book Ezra's Burden. It's completely different from Vegas Baby but worth the read. Any way thanks for your time. I also hope to have Vegas Baby out as a comic book sometime soon, next novel will be called: Vegas Baby and the Crown Royale. Can't wait for you to find about what that's about, until next time!

Thanks again.

C.R. Ward